MOURNING COMMUTE

SAM CHEEVER

ELECTRIC PROSE PUBLICATIONS

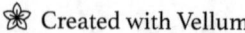 Created with Vellum

It's definitely curtains for May's client. He's exited Stage Left for the last time.

May Ferth just wants to do a good job in her role as a fake girlfriend. But there are strange goings-on at the funeral. Shifty characters whispering secrets in shadowed corners and a truly yummy advocate for the dead guy implying that May might have had something to do with his friend's unscripted exit.

May might be a thirty-three-year-old ex-community theater actress on her second career, but she comes from a family of cops. And, despite her talent for acting, she has a lot more Detective in her than Diva.

The villain thinks he can threaten her and she'll fold like last week's panned play. Clearly, he hasn't read the day's script changes. May and her little dog Shakespeare are on the case. Though, they might take a little direction from the Private Investigator who believes that May's client was murdered and fully intends to prove it.

STAY IN TOUCH

Sam doesn't give away a lot of books. But she values her readers and, to show it, she's gifting you a copy of a fun book just for signing up for her newsletter!

SIGN UP FOR SAM'S NEWSLETTER!

https://samcheever.com/newsletter/

1

Tucking the tiny bottle of fake tears more deeply into my tissue, I sniffed daintily. I surreptitiously eyed the assembled crowd of mourners in an attempt to gauge their feelings about the deceased. In my line of work, it paid dividends to know what I was dealing with when interacting with the mourners. My baby blues caught on a handsome, dark-haired man standing back from the rest, and I quickly jerked my gaze away, hoping he didn't notice me noticing him again.

He totally noticed me.

The man had been staring at me since I'd arrived at the viewing an hour earlier. I would have been pleased by his attention, except that his expression was anything but friendly.

Somehow my eyes kept traveling back to him, all the while assuring myself that it was an accident.

I wasn't ogling the mourners.

Really, I wasn't.

Of its own volition, my gaze accidentally slipped back over the spot where the hostile hottie had been, and I blinked.

He was gone.

To cover my surprise, I turned to the elderly woman next to me and let my bottom lip quiver. I gave a practiced little sob and squeezed the fake tears in my tissue just as a big hand landed on my shoulder.

I yelped, inadvertently gripping the tiny bottle as if it was the only thing keeping me from plunging a thousand feet off a bridge to my death, and then yelped again as I shot a stream of faux sadness right into one wide blue eye.

Fake tears ran like the River Jordan down my artificially pale cheek. "Oh!" I exclaimed as I tried to deal with the mess.

I jerked around to eye the owner of the hand and forgot how to speak.

Across the room he'd been yummy, definitely an eight-star performance on opening night. But up close and personal, Mr. Hostile was a solid fifteen stars, with a good three-minute standing ovation added in.

Even with the glare on his face.

I couldn't help wondering why he seemed so angry

with me. Surely it wasn't because I was ogling him at the viewing of a man who was supposed to have been my boyfriend. I gave that one a few beats of consideration.

Nah. That couldn't be it.

Hostile Hottie stuck the hand he'd accosted me with in front of my face, all but daring me to shake it. "Eddie Deitz."

I blinked. "Huh?" Brilliant, MayBell. Oscar-worthy response.

My poor tissue was swamped with fake tears, and there were more of them trailing down one cheek. I couldn't seem to get them under control. So, I decided to embrace the dramatic substance of the moment. I quivered my bottom lip and sniffled behind the lump of saturated tissue.

Accepting his challenge, I placed a limp paw into his and allowed it to be pumped. "MayBell Ferth. It's a pleasure." Ugh! I wanted to kick myself. Who says that at a funeral? Jeezopete!

The man's gorgeous green gaze narrowed slightly, bringing my attention to the thick fringe of black lashes framing his eyes.

I'd do a year's worth of PiYo classes to have lashes like that. And that was really saying something because I hated PiYo with the power of a thousand suns.

"Is there something wrong with your eye?" he asked.

I mopped ineffectually at the fake tears with my soggy tissue. "Um, no, I'm just sad."

Stupid, May. Stupid.

His expression told me he didn't believe I was sad out of only one eye. I couldn't blame him for his skepticism.

"I don't believe we've met," he said. But even though it sounded for all the world like a come-on, the hostility in his gaze told me it definitely wasn't.

Nodding, I cast a look toward the open casket across the room and sniffled. "Josh and I had only dated a few weeks." I could feel Eddie's gaze on me. It was beyond unfriendly. I couldn't help feeling as if he was accusing me of something.

Like lying about having dated his...Josh.

Mr. Eddie Deitz was looking at me like I'd been caught standing next to Colonel Mustard in the library clutching the bloody murder weapon.

Nerves jangling under his regard, I shoved a loose dark gold curl back into the chignon I'd forced my heavy hair into for the viewing.

"You dated?" he asked, one dark brow peaking in surprise.

My smile was the perfect mix of sad and nostalgic, with a touch of regret thrown in for good measure. "Yes. I'm going to miss him so much." He eyed the lump of soggy tissue in my hand, no doubt noting the way all the fibers had melded together into a single slightly scary science experiment with a telltale, bottle-shaped lump in the center.

"Funny." Eddie Deitz leaned one broad shoulder against the wall, crossing his arms over his well-cut chest. "Josh never mentioned you."

At that point, I was actually pretty proud of my performance. I allowed tears to leak from my eyes—both of them. And took a deep, shaky breath. "Our love was new. Delicate. We weren't talking about it yet."

Scraping the drenched remains of my tissue under my nose, I tried to catch a glimpse of Eddie Deitz from under my lashes. My "not nearly as thick and long as his" lashes.

He was still eyeing me like I should be wearing prison orange.

"Eddie. How are you, son?"

Mr. Deitz and I jerked around to find the father of the deceased heading our way. I was torn between relief and guilt.

Had Mr. Mitner caught me ogling the mourners? Well, to be fair, not every mourner. Just the extremely grumpy Mr. Deitz.

Alex Mitner dropped a hand on my shoulder and squeezed it. I fought the guilt, trying to decipher if the squeeze was a silent reprimand. Something along the lines of, "How dare you molest the mourners when I'm paying you to pretend you're my son's girlfriend."

Had he squeezed a bit harder than necessary?

"How are you holding up, May?"

I let a tear slide from my eyes and nodded, sniffling. The smile I gave him was sad, touched with regret, and had a tinge of romantic longing peppered in for good measure.

I think it was some of my best work.

Mr. Mitner seemed to like it. He gave me another squeeze and nodded as if he understood.

Eddie Deitz didn't look convinced by my performance.

Le sigh... Everybody's a critic.

"I was just telling MayBell that Josh had never mentioned her to me," Deitz said.

Mr. Mitner's mouth turned grim. "I'm sure there were a lot of things you two didn't discuss. You haven't been around much lately."

And just like that, the tension spiked into the stratosphere. I forgot to pretend to mourn for a beat as I looked from one to the other of the two men, trying to read their body language.

It was something that I was pretty good at doing. Excellent really. And I'd credited it with a lot of my success as an actor. I could ascertain the most microscopic emotions in a human expression...decipher the smallest reaction in body language.

I used that information to strengthen the roles I undertook in Community Theater. Or, at least, I had. Until recently, when I quit because I couldn't stand the politics and personal drama anymore. I was currently working for a professional mourning company named Exit Stage Left. It was a much better gig overall. Even if I was occasionally distracted by the motives, emotions, and unwitting cues of the people around the deceased.

Right at that moment, the father of the deceased was rigid with anger, as if he blamed Mr. Deitz for his son's death. And Mr. Deitz seemed cool as a cucumber. Too cool, I thought, given that he'd apparently been close to Joshua Mitner in some capacity.

"I have a job to do, Alex. I'm sorry I couldn't devote every day to babysitting Josh."

My client turned to stone before my very eyes. His fists clenched into boulders at his sides, and his broad jaw transformed to granite. He beamed rage toward a seemingly unconcerned Mr. Deitz.

Apparently, Mr. Eddie Deitz had hostility only for me.

"I'm sure Josh wouldn't have wanted a babysitter," I said before realizing my mistake.

Never, never, never take sides against the client.

Stupid, stupid, May.

What had I done?

Mr. Mitner's granite jaw compressed to diamond-hardness for a moment and then, incredibly, softened. He rubbed a hand over his chin, sighing. "You're right, my dear. I'm so sorry, Ed. That was unfair of me. I'm just so..." Genuine emotion swamped the older man, and his shoulders rounded beneath it. He seemed to crumble before my eyes.

I found myself reaching for him. Wrapping my arms around him and giving him what comfort I could. "I'm so sorry for your loss, Mr. Mitner."

He took a long, shuddering breath and pulled out of my embrace, nodding. Though his steely gray eyes were shiny with tears, he somehow willed the drops not to fall.

Alex Mitner sniffed loudly, dragging a hand under his slightly oversized nose. "Thank you, May. That's very kind of you." Mitner scanned Eddie a quick look and then fixed an intense gaze on me. "Especially since you have your own grief to manage." He held my gaze just a beat longer than necessary, and I caught his message.

I'd veered perilously close to stepping out of character.

Patting his arm, I nodded. "We take comfort being with others who share our pain."

He seemed to like that. Nodding brusquely, he offered Eddie his hand. "Come by the house after? We're just having close friends and family over."

Eddie nodded. "Of course."

We watched him return to his wife, who was so distraught she'd slumped into a chair when they'd first arrived and hadn't risen from it yet. Her face was an unhealthy color, and her eyes were rimmed with red. I was pretty sure she hadn't stopped crying since entering the viewing room.

If I hadn't been warned by Ruthie Colburn, the owner of Exit Stage Left, not to interact with Joshua's mother, I would have felt the need to console her too.

But apparently, Mrs. Mitner wasn't entirely on board with the whole "personal mourner" concept, and it was best not to rub her nose in it.

A warm hand encircled my arm, and I turned to find Eddie staring down at me. He had a look in his eye that concerned me a lot.

Then he smiled, and icy fingers of fear slipped along my spine. "How about you and I go pay our respects to Josh. I don't think I've seen you up there yet."

He hadn't. And dang him, I was hoping he wouldn't. Not that I couldn't do my part with the deceased in the casket. It was just that it was a delicate matter—the core of my performance. I preferred to do it when there's no negativity staining my efforts.

And Mr. Eddie Deitz was about a hundred and eighty pounds of pure negativity.

2

I allowed Eddie to lead me to the casket, the soggy clump of tissue still clutched in my hand and fisted before my mouth for a dual purpose. It was a very effective sign of emotional turmoil, and it kept my fake tears handy in case thinking about gaining ten pounds just before swimsuit season didn't bring real tears to my eyes.

Though that usually worked.

Eddie kept throwing me looks as we approached. I wasn't concerned. Having committed to the role, I was ready for him.

I was ready for anything.

I was super mourner. Hear me cry.

Eddie dropped my arm as we stopped beside the casket. His gaze slipped downward, a bit reluctantly I thought, and softened. One big hand found the side of the casket, and the knuckles turned white.

His jaw tightened and tears shone in his dark green eyes.

I was watching him so carefully, gauging his reaction to seeing Joshua Mitner laid out for the viewing, that I nearly forgot to feign my own grief.

Whatever the relationship between the two men had been, Mr. Eddie Deitz was well and truly mourning Josh's loss.

Without thinking, I reached out and clasped his hand, giving it a squeeze.

He lifted his drenched gaze to mine, surprise flitting quickly through it, and sniffled. "I can't believe he's gone."

I nodded, turning at last to the pale representation of a human lying in the casket.

It was clearly not Josh Mitner. Though I'd never met him in life, the form lying in that casket held nothing of life in its shape and color.

It could just as easily have been a mannequin lying among the cream-colored satin.

Makeup and careful positioning just couldn't mimic the vibrancy of existence. But I understood the need to see him one last time. Even if it wasn't perfect, it was the last chance to say goodbye, to put differences in the past and nurture the love that had been lost.

Unbidden, tears were sliding down my cheeks at the thought. It was one thing to practice pretending to be sad and quite another to be faced with the reality of death and what it did to those who were left behind.

It was the people who'd loved Josh Mitner that I was crying for. My religious upbringing told me he was in a better place and didn't need my tears.

"He looks terrible," Eddie Deitz mumbled.

I swung a shocked gaze his way and saw his wide mouth turn up in a sad smile. "And he'd have been furious to find out they put makeup on him."

I couldn't help chuckling as I nodded my head. I didn't know if it was true, but it certainly seemed likely given his choice of friends.

Of course, Eddie and Josh might not have been friends. They might have been lovers. Or they could have been related somehow. Cousins? But the difference in coloring was vast enough that it seemed unlikely.

Eddie was dark, with smoldering good looks that were only enhanced by his individual features. He had inky black hair combed straight back from a broad forehead and full lips over nearly perfect white teeth. One canine was missing the tip as if he'd been punched in the mouth or had fallen on his face once. Eddie's thick black eyebrows were formed in a permanently judgmental slash over his forest green gaze.

A dark shadow of whiskers covered his jaw. I couldn't tell if it was intentional or because it was after six o'clock in the evening— nature's way of reminding him that he was thoroughly male.

He was a head taller than my own five feet nine and lean, though when he flexed his arm his biceps bulged nicely beneath the white button-down shirt he wore.

By contrast, I knew from photos of the deceased that Josh Mitner had been light-skinned, with pale blue eyes that were over-scored by thick golden brows. His hair had been dark gold and so dense I figured he'd had trouble getting it to lie flat when he'd been alive. He had been about the same height as Eddie Deitz but leaner. Too lean, actually. As if he'd often forgotten to eat. His bio described him as an accomplished athlete, a college basketball star with too much energy to sit still for very long.

Reading between the lines in his dossier, I'd formed a picture in my mind of an unfulfilled man whose existence hadn't satisfied the constant ache for more, which he'd probably grappled with all his life. It was most likely the reason he'd catted around so much, traveling the world and being photographed with too many young women to count.

And why he'd never settled down with any one of them.

"He would have hated the way you're looking at him right now," Eddie said with a smile.

I blinked, wondering what my face had shown

the very observant man. Shaking my head, I dragged the soggy clump of wood pulp that had once been a tissue under one eye. "I was just remembering how he'd been that last day..."

"When was that?" Deitz asked too quickly.

I panicked. I'd said too much. Gone too far. Those kinds of details weren't part of my prep.

Fortunately, I was always over-prepared. "We'd gone to the farmer's market downtown," I told him without missing a beat. "Josh was going to cook me breakfast. Frittatas. With green pepper, onion, and goat cheese."

Eddie's gaze stayed on mine for a beat before he slowly nodded. "He did like to cook."

I didn't respond to that. Less was more. Just in case Josh had secretly confided to Eddie that he hated cooking and only pretended to do it to get girls or something. If it meant he thought I was a sap for love, so be it. I could live with that.

Professionally speaking.

"We never made that breakfast. One thing led to another, and then..." Heat flared in my cheeks. Had I really said that? Good heavens! I'd been reading too many romance novels and had gotten carried away. "I mean..."

Deitz lifted a hand to stop me. "That's okay. I don't need those details."

I had to cover my lips to hide the smile.

"Well..." He suddenly seemed unable to stand there any longer. "It was nice meeting you, May."

I offered him my hand. "It was a pleasure meeting one of Josh's friends. I can see why you two got along."

Deitz held my gaze a moment longer and then frowned. "Funny, I wouldn't have thought you were his type." His eyes narrowed and something passed over his face. It looked like regret. But that made no sense at all.

An awkward silence followed his declaration. I hurried to fill it. "No? Well, love doesn't always make sense, does it?"

"No. It doesn't."

The intensity in his gaze deepened, but I held my ground.

Finally, he said, "Well..." And then he left me, striding quickly toward the door and out.

I expelled the breath I hadn't known I was holding. His perusal of me had been strange. Unlike anything I'd experienced before at one of my mourning jobs. It had almost been like...

I blinked in surprise. No. It had been *exactly* like he'd suspected me of something.

Did Mr. Eddie Deitz really think I might have had something to do with Josh's death?

Surely not.

"Thank you for coming."

I turned at the softly spoken words and found

myself looking down at Mrs. Mitner. She was a small woman, probably not more than five feet three or four inches. There wasn't a lot of extra flesh on her bones either. Like a lot of wealthy women, she probably starved herself and worked out too much, so she looked good in her designer clothes.

But Mrs. Mitner didn't strike me as that type of person. The lack of padding on her small frame was probably more the result of emotional upheaval than deliberate starvation.

I reached out and clasped her hand, trying to capture her gaze. But she kept her watery blue stare pointed downward, toward the floor between our shoes. "I'm so sorry for your loss."

The woman's mouth tightened slightly when she finally looked up. Her stare was hard, and I watched anger flicker through her eyes. "I'm not ashamed of Joshua, you know. I loved my son."

It was such a strange thing to say that all I could do was nod. But the pain sliding through her gaze to replace the fleeting wave of irritation made my chest go tight. I couldn't help adding, "I'm sure he knew."

She skimmed me a look. "Knew?"

"That you loved him."

She sighed softly. "I hope he did. His choices were his own. I never wanted to make him someone other than who he was." Her gaze slipped across the room to where her husband was having a very intense conversation with a smaller man whose balding head seemed to shake too often from side to side and whose dark brown eyes were focused on the casket as they spoke.

I couldn't miss the hostility in her face when Mrs. Mitner glanced at her husband. Had Alex Mitner tried to make their son change his party boy ways?

"Josh would have understood that you only wanted the best for him."

Her delicate jaw tightened. She opened her mouth and spoke to me through gritted teeth. "How would you know? You didn't know our son. You shouldn't even be here. It's an insult to his memory. You're a fake. A fraud."

My stomach jumped at the accusation. It wasn't even her words so much as the venomous way she'd said them. I was in a precarious spot. I didn't want to try to justify my place there. If Mrs. Mitner didn't believe we were doing a good thing, who was I to tell her differently? But I was proud of my work. I was pleased that we made a person's grieving easier. If we gave them a reason to believe their lost loved ones had been happy in their last days...or that they were loved and would be missed...how was that bad?

I inclined my head, speaking softly to the distraught woman. "I know because I've met you and your husband. I can see how much you loved your son. Surely he could have never doubted it himself."

My words seemed to take some of the heat from

her anger. She shook her head. "I can't stay here any longer." She threw her son a last look and, with tears sliding down her pale cheeks, turned away and left the room.

Her leaving left me shaken. I didn't like thinking that I was making her loss harder. That hadn't been the intent at all. But in the end, I was being paid to perform a service. I had just never expected my work to cause more pain rather than less.

It appeared I should have thought of that. After all, everyone I spoke to ran scurrying from the room. I was starting to feel like the pooper of Joshua Mitner's party.

Suddenly, I couldn't stay there either. I glanced toward Mr. Mitner but he was gone, along with the man he'd been speaking to. I looked around and saw nobody I recognized. Nobody seemed interested in me.

I'd fulfilled my obligation for the viewing. I was free to leave.

Then, why did I feel guilty as I headed for the door?

The hallway was nearly empty. I hurried out of the room, heading for the front door. If I was lucky, I could get out of there before Mr. Mitner returned and saw me. Not that he would care if I left, but I was afraid he'd ask me to ride in the limousine with him and his wife to their house.

I couldn't do that to Mrs. Mitner. Her pain was

visceral. For whatever reason, my presence was making it worse.

My shoes were silent on the thick, dark carpeting. I passed three other rooms which fed off the wide hallway. Two of them were empty and dark, the heavy wooden doors closed. In the room nearest the front entrance, the doors were open and the lights were on, but there was nobody inside.

At least, I didn't think anybody was inside. Until I heard the deep rumble of male voices. I skidded to a stop as I recognized Mr. Mitner's voice. He sounded angry.

The other man's tone was placating, his voice soft against the rumble of Alex Mitner's deep voice. "Are you sure he didn't see anything? What if he told somebody?"

"Of course, he didn't say anything. Why would you ask me that? Are you implying Joshua was killed because he found out…?"

"Keep your voice down, Alex."

Alex Mitner expelled air in a frustrated sigh. "I just want this to be over. I want to mourn my son's loss and put it behind me."

"We'll get there," the unknown man said softly. "But you need to keep your wits about you."

"Why are you skulking around the potted plants?"

I jumped, spinning around to find Eddie Deitz smiling at me. "I…I was just…"

"Ms. Ferth? What are you doing?" my client asked.

I closed my eyes briefly, opening them to find Eddie staring at me, curiosity clear in his expression. Forcing a smile, I turned to face Alex Mitner's scowl. "I was just looking for you to tell you I'm leaving."

"You're coming to the house, though right? You need to come to the house."

I could feel Eddie's interest burning along my back. "Yes. Of course. I just have some errands..."

"I'd like you to ride with us," my client said. "In the limo."

"I don't think that's a good idea..." I started to say.

"Just wait a few minutes and we'll go." He started to turn away. I panicked, throwing Eddie a pleading look.

Fortunately, he didn't need a brick to the head to see my plight. "She's going to ride over with me, Alex. She promised to fill me in on what Josh's been doing over the last few months."

Alex Mitner held Eddie's gaze for a long moment and then slid a speculative look my way. With obvious reluctance, he finally nodded. "We'll see you there in an hour?"

"We'll be there," Eddie told him. He clasped my arm gently but firmly and led me to the door.

I couldn't believe my bad luck. I'd managed to escape the frying pan, only to be flung kicking and screaming, right into the dang fire.

3

It turned out the fire analogy was a good one. We hadn't even left the parking lot before Eddie was turning up the heat. "Tell me who you *really* are."

I did my best to look surprised. "I don't know what you mean. I'm Josh's girlfriend..."

He was already shaking his head. "I know that's not true. Tell me who you are."

"Mr. Deitz..."

"Eddie. And just stop it. Don't lie to me. You might have fooled Alex, but you're not fooling me. You're after the Mitner money, aren't you?"

I sat there, staring at him with my mouth hanging unattractively open.

He raised twin dark brows. "Blink once for yes."

He was making fun of me, on top of accusing me of being a thief. It was just too much. "How dare you?"

"I dare because I care." The words were bitter—a self-loathing screed. "I've been MIA in Josh's life for months. I've let him down. I know that now. I should have been involved. I might have been able to help..." Eddie swallowed hard, his lips clamping shut.

Almost angrily, Eddie Deitz turned the key on his ancient blue truck and put it in gear. He didn't say another word until we were in the street and on our way.

To where I didn't know. I only knew that the next hour was probably going to be the longest of my life. "It's not your fault he was killed."

He threw on the brakes as the light turned yellow, his head whipping around. "Oh, I know it wasn't my fault, Miss-Whoever-You-Are. It's yours."

I reared back. "I beg your pardon!"

"You might not have killed him yourself, but you might as well have. People like you—gold-diggers, bloodsuckers—haunted Josh all his life. It's the reason he couldn't be happy, couldn't rest."

"Now you listen to me, Mr. Deitz..."

He opened his mouth to interrupt me again, but I stuck a finger in his face, my Irish coming up in a big way. "No! You put a stinky sock in it and listen to me for a fat second. In the three minutes since we've been in this truck, you've accused me of being a thief, a gold-digger, and a murderer. You don't even know me. You have no idea who I am. You have no right..." Words failed me. As always happened when I was really mad, the tears came. And that made me madder still.

I scraped a hand under my eyes and sniffled. "Why am I bothering? You've made up your mind already. You're not even listening to me."

We were on the move again, heading out of town toward the oversized feet of the Smoky Mountains. I was pretty sure the Mitners lived in the other direction.

His hostility softening just a bit, Eddie handed me a tissue. "Well, at least this time, the tears are real."

And there it was. I was not only a thief, a murderer, and a gold-digger, but I was also a lousy actress. I sat there shaking with rage. The man was the worst kind of... I blinked as I realized where we were. He'd taken me to the last place I wanted to go.

Eddie pulled the truck to the side of the road and turned it off. He sat staring at the simple cross stuck into the ground next to the road. Someone had recently placed fresh flowers on the marker. They hadn't even started to wilt in the metal vase yet. The debris had been cleaned away. Only the broken stop sign indicated that anything had even occurred there.

I swallowed the sudden lump in my throat. It was one thing to play at knowing the deceased and quite another to learn the painful details of his death. I was suddenly afraid to hear them. "We should really get back. The Mitners will be wondering…"

Eddie opened the door and climbed out. He walked around to the front of the truck and headed for the intersection. Before I knew what I was doing, I was climbing out too, toddling along behind him in my three-inch-tall heels. "Eddie? What are you doing? You should get back in the truck."

He shoved his hands into his pockets and kept walking as if I wasn't even there. He stopped in front of the tilting sign, his gaze focused in the direction the truck that had hit Josh had probably come from.

I stopped beside him and waited for him to give me some indication of what he was doing. I didn't have long to wait.

"He always drove too fast," Eddie murmured. "But he knew this road like the back of his hand. He drove it day and night, rain or snow. Drunk or sober…" The words were strangled under a soft sob.

I touched his arm, offering what little support I could. "Don't do this to yourself, Eddie."

He shook his head, tears sliding down his cheeks. "I should have been here."

"And what?" I asked him. "Would you have been driving? Would he have listened to you if you'd been a passenger? Would you have realized that a big truck was heading for the exact spot where his car was going to be?"

Deitz sniffed, looking down the road as he struggled to get his emotions under control.

"This Stop sign is hard to see. Even if you know it's here, if you're distracted or not paying attention, it could sneak up on you. It was dark that morning, right? He was heading to work very early?"

Eddie nodded. "He hated working there. Hated the way his dad treated him. And the way everybody looked at him because they all thought he was skating through life." Eddie gave a bitter laugh. "Josh was a player. He was unreliable and flighty. But he was one of the kindest, gentlest men I knew."

"He was your friend," I said softly.

"Yeah." He turned to look me in the eye.

His tone of voice should have warned me. But I was still caught up in the heart-breaking trail of pain Joshua Mitner's death had left behind.

"And that's why I know you're not his girlfriend. He would have mentioned you to me. But he never did, May...or whatever your real name is...he never mentioned you even one time. How do you explain that?"

I couldn't. And even if I could have come up with a plausible reason, I knew Eddie Deitz wouldn't buy it. He was shrewd, and he paid attention to even the smallest details. I recognized the trait from my family, most of whom were cops.

I was the rare breed of Ferth who'd eschewed law

enforcement for a life pretending to be someone I wasn't.

That was probably why I understood Josh's mindset. Maybe better even than his friend Eddie could. I realized I had a choice to make. I could break my contract and tell Eddie what I was doing there. Or I could continue to lie to him and go on being a suspect in his eyes.

I really had no choice. "I told you, Eddie. I was Josh's girlfriend. I can't tell you why he didn't talk about me. It actually hurts my feelings a little bit."

He stalked closer, his jaw tight and his hands clenched into fists. "You're going to tell me the truth. I won't stop asking."

I raised my hands, backing toward the truck. "What is your deal?" I asked. I let him see my fear, hoping he'd come to his senses...become more reasonable. Unfortunately, I was pretty sure Eddie Deitz had passed reasonable a while back and would have trouble finding it again.

I bumped up against the truck. Nowhere to go. He pushed his face to within a few inches of mine, well past my comfort zone. Eddie jabbed a finger at me, making me blink. "The only reason I can see for you to lie is if you have something to hide. I don't know exactly what you're up to, but I know you're working for somebody else. Somebody who wanted Josh dead. I'm going to find out who. When I do, I'm taking you down for his murder."

I grabbed his finger and pushed it out of my face, finally as angry as he was. "Don't you threaten me, Deitz! I had nothing to do with Josh's death."

"We'll just see about that, won't we?"

"Yes, we will." I turned away from him and started down the road, wobbling in my heels.

"May!"

I ignored him, dialing my brother the cop. Of course he didn't answer.

Gravel crunched behind me, and my hand stabbed into my purse. As he grabbed my shoulder, I spun around and sprayed him right in the face with mace.

Eddie screamed and raged, mopping at his stinging eyes and calling me just about every kind of villain he could imagine. I phoned my dad, who was also a cop and got through. "Dad, I need you to come get me." I cut Eddie Deitz a look and found him squint-staring at me, looking like a zombie with his fire engine red eyes. "I'll explain when you get here."

"You need to get a safer job, Punkin. Maybe you should become a cop."

I gave my dad the patented Ferth female "look" that was supposed to drop him to his knees. Unfortunately, he'd grown immune to the Ferth equivalent of stink eye and didn't even wobble.

"I'm serious. I think there's something strange about Joshua Mitner's death."

Police Lieutenant George Ferth signaled and turned onto my road, his distinguished, still handsome face wrinkling with dismay. "Based on a whispered conversation between the father and some guy you don't even know? Punkin, that guy could be a weird uncle who borrowed money and didn't return it. It could have nothing at all to do with this young man's death."

"I can't explain why I feel this way. It's just my gut."

He skimmed a look over my flat tummy and smirked. "Punkin, you don't have a gut. You've got skin stretched tightly over bones and not much else. You need to come home for dinner more often."

"Lieutenant," I whined. That one always got him.

He shook his head, pulling up in front of my apartment building. "All right. I'll read the report on the crash. But don't get your hopes up. From what I've heard about it, that boy died in a tragic accident. He was quite the party boy, you know. There's a good chance he was drunk and just didn't notice the Stop sign."

"It was like six in the morning, Dad."

He shrugged. "Your point?"

I grasped the handle and pushed the door open. "Thanks for coming to get me."

"Any time, Punkin. What was the deal with that

guy in the truck, anyway? Was he inappropriate with you?" The Lieutenant's bulldog jaw tightened, and his hands fisted around the steering wheel of his Escalade.

"No. He's actually a friend of the deceased. I think he believes I killed Josh." My pulse spiked as I said the words out loud. I still couldn't believe it.

The Lieutenant's shaggy brows lifted with disbelief. He stared at me for a long moment, and I wondered what he was thinking. I'd never been able to read his expressions.

Finally, the brows returned to their normal spot on his face, and he started laughing. A deep, endorphin-raising belly laugh that went on for a full minute. He swiped tears from his eyes and shook his head. "Well, *he's* stupid."

"He's not stupid, Dad. He's..." I frowned as my mind searched for the right adjective. I finally settled on one that kind of worked. "He's intense."

"Intense, huh? What is Mr. Intense basing this ridiculous belief on?"

"Because he doesn't know who I am, and I was at the funeral pretending to be Josh's girlfriend."

The Lieutenant chewed on that one for a minute. "Okay, I can see that. But it's still a leap."

"I know. Like I said, he's intense."

"There's more to it. Isn't there?" The Lieutenant had his own version of the evil eye and his worked a lot better than mine. I shifted uncomfortably in my seat.

"I might have been sizing up all the mourners and skulking around behind a potted palm."

The Lieutenant shook his head. "You should have been a cop, Punkin. You can't seem to help yourself."

I shrugged. Deep down, I knew he was right. The problem was, I didn't want to be a cop. I wanted to be an actor.

"Well, I'll give him points for hanging around with you until I picked you up. Even if he was hiding in his truck when I got there."

Despite myself, I couldn't quite repress the grin fighting to escape. My lips quivered. "Especially after I pepper-sprayed him."

The Lieutenant barked out a laugh. "That's my girl. Come to the house for dinner soon. Y'hear?"

"Yes, sir. I will," I promised him. Blowing him a kiss, I watched him pull into traffic and roar off, tackling the road like he did everything else.

Full speed ahead and darn the torpedoes.

I was unlocking my front door before I realized I'd completely spaced on the Mitner wake at their home. "Dangit!"

I dropped my purse on the table by the door and called out to the yipping Pomeranian Devil in the back room. "I'll be right there, Shakespeare!"

"Dangit, dangit, dangit!"

Grabbing my phone, I dialed Exit Stage Left, praying the owner, Ruthie Colburn would be in a forgiving mood. My situation definitely required a prayer because hope wasn't nearly strong enough.

Ruthie didn't cotton to shenanigans and tomfoolery. Unless, of course, it made her money.

I chewed on my lip, trying to ignore the frantic yipping coming from my bedroom, and waited for the phone to ring several times. Ruthie finally answered on the seventh ring, just when I was about to give up.

"May! My gosh, what's your hurry?" Ruthie gave a watery cough, sounding like a two-pack-a-day smoker. She wasn't. And had never been as far as I knew. But she definitely had the voice of one.

Since the rings hadn't happened any faster than usual, I wasn't sure why I'd been labeled an unnecessary rusher, but it didn't matter because in a minute she was going to have something to really be irritated with me about. "Hey, Ruthie."

"Shouldn't you be standing in the Mitner's living room right now, pretending you aren't hungry and drinking only water despite a strong hankerin' for a whiskey neat?"

I stood there blinking for a minute before she said, "Oh, sorry, that last part was me. Why are you calling me instead of standing in the Mitner's living room looking sad?"

"I uh...well..."

"Spit it out, girl!" she barked in her painful sounding rasp.

"I was kind of attacked by one of the mourners."

Ruthie went very quiet, no doubt calculating how much it would cost her if I complained or, *gasp*, decided to press charges.

"It's not dire. But he's convinced himself I killed the deceased, and he kind of kidnapped me." Okay, I was exaggerating a tad, but I needed Ruthie to understand how desperate I was when I admitted how I'd pepper-sprayed him.

"May, why would he think you killed the guy you were supposed to love?"

"He totally wasn't buying my girlfriend act!" Then I realized Ruthie would see that as a failure to portray on my part and quickly went on. "He didn't know who I was, and he thought he would if I was really Josh's girlfriend. He wasn't even convinced when Josh's father backed up my story. *See, Ruthie, he didn't believe the client either. I can act. Really, I can.*

"Tell me what happened."

I told her about Mrs. Mitner's hysterics and Mr. Mitner's determination to get me into that dang limo and Eddie saving me by offering to drive me to the house and then not driving me to the house and taking me to the intersection where Josh had been killed to accuse me of murder instead.

By the time I got to the pepper spray, Ruthie was

probably already in a coma and hopefully didn't even notice.

I took a deep breath and chewed my lip waiting.

"Pepper spray, May?"

"I know. I panicked. I'm sorry! But it wouldn't be out of character for Josh's girlfriend to spray him. I didn't blow my role."

"You think you can still pull this off?"

"Absolutely."

She sighed, then barked out another wet cough. "Okay, I'll call over there and tell them you came down with a migraine. But you're going to have to really bring it home at the gravesite tomorrow."

"I will, I promise." I hung up, sagging with relief.

Yip, yip, yip!

Shakespeare! I pushed weariness aside and headed for the kennel beside my bed, a.k.a. the Pom Hilton. My poor Pomeranian Devil was probably just about splitting a bladder.

4

___

My doorbell rang as I was settling Shakespeare's bowl down on the floor of the kitchen. The little gray dog gave my fingers a quick lick before sticking his tiny nose into the bowl and daintily picking out some kibble to chew.

I groaned softly as the bell's strident tones rang through my apartment. I was beat. It had been a long, emotionally charged day.

I just wanted to climb into my comfies and cuddle with Shakes in front of the television.

Alas, it wasn't to be. The bell pealed through my apartment again and, food forgotten, Shakes ran barking to answer it.

I had no choice but to follow.

I scooped up the tiny, gray furball at the door and held him as he nearly vibrated out of my arms. Shakes was excitable. But his cascade of a tail was wagging in a friendly way when I pulled the door open to face the person with the annoying doorbell trigger finger.

I nearly swallowed my tongue. Unlike my dog, *my* tail was decidedly not wagging and I was wondering if I could get to my mace before he grabbed me.

As if reading my mind, Eddie Deitz raised his hands. "Don't shoot! I'm not here to cause trouble. I just want to talk."

"How'd you get my address?"

He looked at his feet. "I have my ways."

"Now you're a stalker?" My voice screeched across the space between us. The door to the apartment next door opened, and my harmlessly friendly neighbor Doug stuck his dread-head out into the hall. "Everything okay, Dude?"

I shifted Shakes to my other arm so I could reach toward my purse on the table while eying my intruder. "I'm not sure. Is everything okay, Mr. Deitz?"

Eddie's eyes were hidden behind dark sunglasses. The glasses were oversized and looked like they belonged to a woman. He reminded me of a large, predatory bug standing there. Except he was much cuter than a bug. "I promise, I don't want any trouble."

I stared meaningfully at him for a moment and then looked at Doug. "I think I'm okay. But if I turn up dead in a field somewhere, this guy's name is Eddie Deitz. He was the last person to see me before I was gacked."

"Dude!" Doug nodded briskly, threw Eddie a vacant look and closed the door, leaving behind the suspicious scent of burning leaves.

Eddie lifted a brow. "Gacked? Really?"

I shrugged. "What do you want?"

"I want you to come to the wake. Alex is beside himself that you're not there."

Shakes stretched his tiny nose into the hallway, whining a greeting to the bespectacled intruder. His tail smacked the back of my arm with happy regularity.

"You're kidding, right? I'm not getting back in a car with you."

"Look, I'm sorry. I'm not taking Josh's death well. I might have overreacted."

"Might?" I lifted my brows in amazement. "You accused me of killing him."

Eddie dipped his head. "Maybe that was a tad hysterical." The slow, crooked smile transported his face from handsome to stunning. It had an actual physical effect on me.

Still, I hesitated.

He expelled air. "Look, I'd have to be crazy to do anything to Lieutenant Ferth's daughter, wouldn't I?"

"How do you know who my father is?" I narrowed my gaze.

"I saw him when he came to pick you up."

"You know him?"

"*Know* is too strong of a word. We've...um...interacted before."

"Please tell me my father didn't arrest you."

"Your father didn't arrest me."

"Why don't I believe you?"

"I have no idea. I'm an honest guy, trust me."

"Yeah, see, that whole 'trust you' thing has already bitten me in the butt. I'm not in a real big hurry to do it again."

"Okay, then trust that I'm terrified of your dad, and there's always Doug. I mean...Dude...he'll tell on me if anything happens to you."

I couldn't help it. I grinned. "Okay, come on in. But I have this..." I held up the canister I'd pulled from my purse. "And I'm not afraid to use it."

I turned and went back inside, settling Shakes onto the floor so he could run and greet the intruder. I watched carefully as Mr. Eddie Deitz crouched down and scratched my little dog behind the ears. Shakes really seemed to like him.

A definite point in his favor.

"He's a handsome little fella. What's his name?"

"Shakespeare."

Deitz looked at me over the glasses. I winced at the vibrant maroon hue of his eyes. "That's a mighty big name for such a little dog."

"He lives up to it, believe me." I turned around

and headed for my bedroom to change. "As long as you're going to be here, make yourself useful. I didn't get a chance to fill his water bowl before. It's on the floor in the kitchen."

"Yes, ma'am."

I grinned as he snapped a hand to his forehead in a military-style salute. I didn't mind being saluted. It complemented my bossy disposition.

"Why'd you name your dog Shakespeare?"

I swung my gaze from the passing Asheville, North Carolina countryside, which was looking a bit brown and wilty in the summer heat. We really needed some rain, and it didn't look as though we were going to get it any time soon. "I got him the day I was chosen to perform the role of Gertrude in the play Hamlet."

He stared at me over the silly-looking glasses. "You're a little young to be Gertrude, aren't you?"

"I'm thirty-three if you're fishing. And a good portrayal is ageless."

He shook his head.

"Where'd you get those glasses? Please tell me they aren't yours."

I'd meant to take a whack at him because he had me feeling peevish and defensive. I always got peevish when I thought or talked about my time in community theatre. I'd been a decent enough stage actress. But I didn't have the temperament for all the drama. I'm not talking about the performing kind of drama. It was the behind-the-scenes kind that robbed me of my chi—the hysterical crying and crystal flinging type of drama.

I'd bumped up against one too many divas and a few too many casting couch wannabes and finally decided to walk. Exit Stage Left had seemed the perfect compromise to my love of acting but distaste for actors. I got to play a role that consoled people in their time of sadness, and I didn't have to dodge cut crystal tumblers thrown by aging, jealous actresses.

Win, win.

"They were actually left in my office by a client. I've been carrying them around with the expectation that I'd return them to her, but I haven't gotten around to it."

"You don't have your own sunglasses?"

"I do. But they're not dark enough." He pulled the bug glasses down and I winced. His eyes were bloodshot and rimmed in deep red. Even the area around the eyes was the color of new blood. "Sorry about that."

He shrugged and said something that gained him my respect. "Don't be. I deserved it."

We drove in silence for a few minutes. The countryside gradually turned less country and more civilized, though it was still dominated by large green areas. The main difference being that the green was decidedly more controlled, and the trees more carefully tended. After another mile, the open spaces started to be enclosed, mostly in tall wrought iron and stone fencing. Gates kept driveways private, and security signs peppered the area around them.

"I guess the Mitners have money," I murmured. There was no judgment in my tone. It was simply an observation.

Eddie looked at me a little funny. "I'm surprised you didn't know that, dating Josh and all."

I could have smacked myself for the rooky mistake. Shrugging in what I hoped was an unconcerned way, I tried to minimize the damage. "I knew *he* had money, but I just figured it was because he had a good job. Josh wouldn't talk about his family much. I only knew they lived in Asheville, but nothing else."

He seemed to be weighing my answer. If he didn't buy it, he didn't let on. "They're good people, the Mitners. Josh was kind of wild. But he was a good man."

It was said softly, no doubt spurred by emotions Eddie probably wouldn't display in front of me. "Why did you imply Josh was murdered?"

"Because he was. I can't prove it yet, but I intend to."

I chewed the inside of my lip, debating whether I

should tell him what I overheard at the funeral home.

"What is it?"

I looked over. He'd taken off the bug glasses and was giving me a raccoon-ish but intense look.

"I wasn't going to tell anybody this, but..."

He eased the truck to a stop at a four-way intersection and turned to me. "What?"

"I overheard Mr. Mitner talking to that other man. It's what I was doing when you found me skulking around that potted palm."

"Why were you eavesdropping?"

I hadn't expected the question, but I supposed it was a fair one. "I hadn't meant to. I was actually leaving, and I heard raised voices in that empty viewing room. I recognized Mr. Mitner's voice and I...well...I was curious."

Eddie frowned. "You were curious?"

I nodded. "It's a side effect of having cops in the family, I guess. We tend to be nosy."

He chuckled. "I can see that. What did you hear while nestled in the prickly arms of the potted palm?"

His tone was light, but I could tell my answer was important to him.

"Not much, really. Mr. Mitner seemed to be worried about something Josh might have heard. And the other guy was assuring him he didn't hear anything. The only reason I paid attention was because they seemed to be kind of hiding away in that other room."

"That's a strange conversation to be having at Josh's viewing."

"Yeah. I thought so too."

He hit the gas and we moved on down the road. Five minutes later, he turned into a gated drive. We were ushered through by a man dressed like CIA. My head swiveled to watch the man as we drove past. I wondered if he had a gun under that dark suit coat. "Do they always have guards at the gate?"

"Not usually. I'd guess he's just there to keep the gate open for guests."

Since that made perfect sense, I put it out of my mind. I had too many other things to consider. First of which was the fact that Eddie still hadn't told me why he thought Josh had been murdered.

And I intended to get that information from him. What could I say? Cop kid. Nosy.

5

Alex Mitner met us at the door, his face an unhealthy shade of gray. He scrubbed a shaky hand over his face and nodded toward the adjoining room, which was filled with people who spoke in soft, deferential tones.

Toward the back of the house, a woman could be heard crying inconsolably. My heart broke for Josh's grieving mother. My gaze caught Mr. Mitner's. "I'm so sorry."

He shook his head. "The doctor just gave her something to help her rest." Alex Mitner looked at Eddie and his expression hardened. "You'll find out who did this?"

Eddie didn't hesitate. "You know I will, sir."

At that moment, I realized there was more to Mr. Eddie Deitz than I realized. I also comprehended that Eddie wasn't the only one who believed Josh was murdered.

The door opened behind us, and Mr. Mitner excused himself to greet his new guests.

I looked at Eddie. "What did he mean by that?"

Eddie eyed me, seemingly weighing whether he should open up to me or not. I waited. If he still believed I'd killed Josh, he probably wouldn't have brought me to the wake. Finally, he grabbed my arm and urged me toward a room where there was a long table filled with food.

The room was uninhabited. He tugged me to the back corner, next to a huge china cabinet built of some kind of rich-looking dark wood. Lowering his head, Eddie spoke to me in soft tones, despite the fact that we were alone in the large room.

"I'm more than Josh's friend. I'm also a private investigator. I've been deep on assignment for a few weeks, doing some legwork for a new client. When I heard Josh was dead, I dumped my caseload to figure out who'd killed him."

"Why do you assume it was anything but an accident?"

"There are things I can't tell you."

I frowned. "You pulled me in here to tell me nothing?"

He grabbed a plate off the nearby buffet, handing it to me. "No. I came in here because I was hungry. Aren't you?"

I rolled my eyes. "You're impossible."

"I'm slightly less impossible when I'm not hungry." He started filling up his plate, and I did a mental shrug. I was there. Food was there with me. I might as well have some of the food. I made a concerted effort not to pile too much onto my plate. A grieving girlfriend probably wouldn't fix herself a plate fit for a lumberjack like Deitz was doing.

Besides, I could always come back for seconds when nobody was looking.

I was stuffing a tiny cheesecake in my face so that I didn't have to put it on my plate where it was in danger of mixing with the sausage lasagna I'd just heaped on there when the small, balding man from the funeral home potted palm incident walked into the room. He jolted to a stop as I sucked cheesecake down the wrong pipe.

I hacked, choked, and coughed explosively as Eddie smacked me hard on the back.

The man by the door burst into motion. He hurried over and grabbed a glass off the buffet, filling it with water from a crystal pitcher and handing it to me. "Drink this."

I gave him a jerky nod and succumbed to another violent bout of coughing before I could get a few sips of the water down.

A few minutes later, I was feeling better and was able to talk. Though my voice sounded strained and rough. "Thanks for the water."

The little man gave me a smile. "That happens to me all the time. Usually, it's when I'm eating too quickly." He lifted an accusing brow and I coughed again, trying and failing for a pity pass.

I *had* been shoveling those little cheesecakes pretty fast behind Eddie's back. I didn't want him to know I was a sugar and fat girl.

Eddie held his hand out to the other man. "Doctor Leland. How's Val?"

I knew from my Exit Stage Left dossier that Val was Valerie Mitner, Josh's mom. But I hadn't realized the man who'd been sharing secrets with Val's husband was apparently their personal physician. That made their whispered conversations take on a different tone altogether.

"She's finally resting. The poor woman's taking her son's death really hard."

I frowned. It would be a strange woman indeed who didn't. "It's truly a tragedy," I said, dabbing at a nonexistent tear in my eye with my linen napkin.

Doctor Leland offered me his hand. "We met at the funeral home."

He did one of those hand over and under things that didn't allow me to retrieve my hand when we were done shaking. I tried to ignore the way his thumb swept over the inside of my wrist.

"We did," I admitted with a guilty flush. I gave my hand an experimental tug. Nope. Not getting it back any time soon. "I'm May Ferth. Josh and I were dating."

Leland swept Eddie a quick look, and I turned to find Eddie's expression snapping back to neutral from something else.

What secret was I not in on that everybody else knew? It was starting to make me cranky.

"Well. How nice." Leland finally dropped my hand. "I always said the boy had good taste." He winked at me.

If I'd been snarfing mini cheesecakes, I'd probably have choked to death on the spot.

Leland headed over to the buffet and grabbed a plate. Eddie and I took that as our cue to skedaddle. He put a hand in the small of my back and urged me into the hallway. The noise from the front of the big house had doubled; voices were no longer subdued. Someone had turned up the music, and it was starting to sound more like a party than a wake.

Eddie steered me toward the back of the house and into what looked like a family room, with comfortable leather furniture and a television as big as one of my living room walls. A pair of pretty French doors on an outside wall led to a patio lit with strands of clear lights.

We stepped outside. The sounds of the crowd inside the house faded to the distant background. It was replaced by the soothing sound of crickets and, somewhere in the distance, the throaty croak of a bullfrog.

The night was warm, and the air smelled like rain. Beyond the softly glowing lights, the sky was a leaden mass that looked volatile.

Sure enough, as I glanced upward, a shot of light speared the bank of clouds in the distance.

"Looks like we're finally going to get some relief from this drought," Eddie told me as he indicated a comfy-looking reclining chair. We settled down next to a softly rippling pool, the water a pretty blue under the lights.

"I heard we're five inches below normal for the year."

It was so easy to fall into discussions of the weather. I could talk to a complete stranger about the lack of rain or the overwhelming heat of a summer day. But Eddie and I weren't going to be allowed to hide behind easy topics. We had a murder to discuss.

"What do you suppose Mr. Mitner and Doctor Leland could have been inferring about Josh?"

Eddie popped a bite of meatloaf into his mouth and chewed. He shook his head as he grabbed a hunk of bread. "I'm not aware of Alex being sick, but if he is, I guess they could have been worried Josh found out about it."

"Why would that matter now?"

"I don't know. None of this makes sense." Eddie stopped eating and seemed to lose interest in his food. He set the plate aside on a small table. "I spoke to Josh minutes before he died. I was probably the last person to talk to him."

"How did he sound?" Despite the charade of my pretending to date Josh, I found I really wanted to know about my pretend boyfriend's last moments. Maybe because of the way it affected the man sitting next to me.

Eddie shrugged. "He sounded happy. He was razzing me about working too much. He said there was a party this weekend..." Eddie swallowed, his gaze locked on the pool. "There was always a party with Josh." He shook his head. "Even if I hadn't been working, I probably wouldn't have gone. That makes me sad."

"I'm sure Josh understood why. You're different people. With different motivations."

Eddie didn't respond. Finally, without looking at me, he asked, "Did he ever talk to you about me?"

I wanted to curl up and hide. It was one thing to play a role. To pretend to be someone I wasn't because that was my job. But to lie to someone I was starting to kind of sort of maybe like...a man who was making himself painfully vulnerable by asking... It was suddenly too much. I opened my mouth, ready to confess.

Eddie didn't give me a chance. "Your silence is my answer." He sounded so sad it nearly broke my heart.

In desperation, I dragged him back to the phone call with Josh. "What did you talk about with Josh that morning?" My intention was pure distraction. I really didn't expect to gather any useful information.

"He was telling me about the woman who was having the party. He met her at the gym, I guess." Eddie gave a snort of laughter. "Josh made friends everywhere he went. And everybody he met was an instant bestie. But he forgot them just as easily, which made for some really awkward moments when old dates approached him."

"I'll bet."

"Then he told me he needed to go because..." Eddie sat up straight in his chair. "He said there was a call he had to take." He looked at me. "Maybe the call was tied to the crash."

I frowned. "You mean he crashed because he was talking on the phone, not paying attention?"

"No, maybe it was the killer." He turned in the lounger and put his feet on the ground. His mind was clearly focused on the dark intersection of that fateful, pre-dawn morning. "Eddie didn't usually travel on that particular road in the mornings. He went that way a lot at night, heading to the bars in Asheville. But to go to work, he usually took the highway. I wondered why he was traveling that particular road when he was killed."

"You're thinking maybe he received a call from somebody telling him to go somewhere, so he changed his route? Where could he have been heading?" I asked.

Eddie stood up and started to pace. "An early morning meeting with one of his bar buddies, maybe?" He shrugged. "Josh was friends with several of the bar owners. Ultimately, the destination didn't matter. It was the route that mattered to the killer. A route that took him through a particular intersection."

"It's a good theory. But it's still just a theory, right?"

"It's more than a theory. I believe Josh was lured to the spot where he was killed."

"How do you know that?"

He hesitated, clearly trying to decide if he should tell me, and then sat back down, resting his arms on his knees as he leaned closer and lowered his voice. "The truck that hit him. The witness said she thought it looked like a trash truck. But I talked to the trash hauling company, they aren't missing a truck, and none of their people reported an accident that morning."

"Maybe their people are lying."

"Did you see the wreckage of Josh's car?"

I flinched, shaking my head.

"There's no way, even a truck as heavy as a trash hauler could demolish a car like that, and both the truck and the driver leave the scene without some evidence that it happened." He suddenly stood up. "I need to get Josh's phone." He started for the house and stopped, turning back. "Wait here. I'll take you home after I get it."

I realized I really needed to mingle a bit, but Eddie was gone before I could tell him I should stick around a while. I decided to wait for him to return and then tell him.

I wasn't stalling or anything. Of course I wasn't.

Though it was really pleasant out there next to the pool, with the potent scent of rain filling the air.

I picked at the food on my plate, taking care to eat very small bites so I didn't choke again. Everything tasted like sawdust, so I set the plate back down. Talking about Josh's horrible death had made my stomach twist.

A breeze slid past, filled with moisture that hadn't resolved to become rain yet. I decided I'd better go inside. I'd do some mingling and then find Eddie.

A small tree next to the pool house shimmied. I narrowed my gaze at it. Was there a dog or something in there? "Hello?"

Nothing.

I did a mental shrug and turned away, picking up

my plate and Eddie's. A brisk wind flashed past and the lights flickered off. The area was barely lit by illumination from inside the house. Lightning flashed again, followed almost immediately by thunder.

The storm was close.

Quick footsteps sounded on the concrete behind me as I turned toward the house. Before I could turn around, a heavy body slammed into me, and the plates of food went flying, crashing onto the patio blocks a few feet away.

I yelped as an arm snaked around my throat. The grip tightened like an iron band, making it hard to breathe. My hands clawed at the arm, my feet scrabbling on the stones for a moment before my panicked brain told me to kick my attacker's shins.

I connected on the second attempt, pleased by the resulting grunt of pain. But the arm around my throat tightened, cutting off all air.

I went very still.

"Tell your partner to keep his nose out of this, or it's going to go very badly for you both."

Before my brain could even make sense of the harshly whispered command, the arm straightened from around my throat and my attacker shoved me hard. My feet left the ground, and I flew through the air.

I hit the pool hard, a solid belly flop that stung

the inadequate amount of air in my lungs right out of me.

Light flared overhead, followed by a teeth-rattling boom, and my feet hit the bottom of the pool as a shadow fell over the water, and something crashed down into the frothy water on top of me.

6

A hundred tiny branches tangled around me, catching in my hair and stabbing through my clothes. I shoved desperately at them, trying to get loose, but they bent without breaking, leaving me stuck like a pincushion and fighting to keep from being shoved to the bottom of the pool.

My lungs were screaming as I finally managed to rip a thick strand of hair loose from one of the bigger branches. I kicked against the bottom but was jerked violently back down. My mouth opened on a small sound of pure terror, my chest on fire.

Glancing down, I saw that a branch as thick as one of my fingers had impaled my blouse, and I wasn't going anywhere until I wrenched it free.

I clasped the wet fabric, yanking as hard as I could, but the water made it both slippery and strong, impossible to break with my bare hands.

Panic swirled in my chest, building with the pressure in my lungs as getting air became the only imperative.

A solution danced just beyond my understanding, too much for my oxygen-starved brain to grasp.

There were several loud splashes above my head. I was dimly aware of dark forms shooting like arrows in my direction.

The blouse wouldn't come free, and the branch was too thick to break. I'd begun to thrash, giving in to panic, when a pair of hands found my shoulder and another grasped the branches holding me under water.

Between the two men, I was yanked from side to side, their efforts to release me not much better than my own.

Without warning, Eddie slipped his hand between the buttons of my blouse and yanked, ripping it open. We fought to pull my arms out of the sleeves. Then, finally, I was free.

Still, if Eddie hadn't been there to help me get to the surface, I don't know if I could have managed it.

My legs and arms were weak from fighting with the tree and lack of oxygen.

We burst from the surface of the pool—me, Eddie, and another guy who looked strong enough to break the tree apart by himself.

Somebody grabbed my wrists and pulled me from the water. Somebody else wrapped me in an oversized towel. And I found myself being led into the house and taken to a bedroom on the first floor.

Valerie Mitner shoved my rescuers out of the room and closed the door. She turned a red-rimmed gaze my way and frowned. "You're very lucky they found you in time." She almost didn't sound happy about that.

I couldn't answer. My teeth were too busy clacking together.

She took another look at me and seemed to take pity. "I think I have something in here you can wear home."

Josh's mother rummaged around in the closet for a minute and came out with a velour tracksuit that looked like it might cover one of my legs. I eyed it doubtfully. I wasn't a whole lot taller than Mrs. Mitner, but my curvy form would definitely test the limits of the tracksuit.

She laid it on the bed, eyeing it dubiously. "Well, at least it's stretchy." She glanced at my bare feet. "I'm afraid I don't have much in the way of shoes for you. My feet are smaller." She disappeared into the closet for a minute and came back out with some-thing, placing them on the bed with the velour. Then she headed for the door. "Get dressed and I'll have Eddie take you home."

She stopped with her hand on the knob, her head lowered. I waited for her to speak, knowing that whatever she wanted to say was dragging her down and she needed to say it.

After a long moment, she finally looked up, her red-rimmed eyes meeting mine. "I'm sorry. I know you're just doing a job. But Josh wasn't a job to me. He was my pride and joy. He was every-thing..." Her voice broke. She closed her mouth, her eyes downcast, and finally nodded. "Thank you for coming tonight. I know I haven't made it easy."

She was gone before my oxygen-deprived brain could come up with a response. I wanted to kick myself for not giving her back some comfort.

Moving stiffly, I pulled off the sopping wet towel and dropped it to the carpet. My drenched skirt and soggy underwear were next. The velour fit me like a second skin. Literally. The top was zippered, and I didn't have anything to wear underneath it. The result was barely decent.

I looked at my bare feet. My favorite open-toed dress shoes were lying at the bottom of the Mitner's pool.

They'd never be the same again.

Then I cast my gaze on the shoes Mrs. Mitner had added to the velour. I grimaced. "Revenge footwear," I muttered as I slipped them on.

I picked up the towel and went to the adjoining bathroom to drape it over the side of the tub. I wrapped my bra and underwear in my once cute short black skirt and, taking a bracing breath, I headed for the door.

Eddie was standing in the hallway, dripping onto the hardwood floor. He looked worried. "Are you okay?" He reached for a sopping ribbon of my wavy, dark gold hair and gave it a gentle tug. "That tree really had a grip on you."

I nodded, my teeth still clacking together. "I'm fine. I just want to go home."

Wrapping an arm around my shoulders, he walked me down the hall.

As we neared the front door, another towel-draped figure emerged from the area where the guests had been. I noticed the house was all but empty and wondered if my unscheduled dunking had anything to do with that.

The man who came toward us was tall and broad-shouldered, with thick dark hair, olive-toned skin, expressive brown eyes and a wide, square jaw that sported a chin dimple. He was gorgeous.

"Is she okay?" he asked Eddie. Then he smiled at me and I felt my knees go weak.

"I'm fine," I managed to stutter between clanking teeth.

"I need to get her home, James."

I giggled. "Home, James..." My teeth clacked loud enough to rattle my brain. I slammed my lips closed.

"She's a little punchy from lack of oxygen, I

think."

James nodded. "We weren't introduced before," he told me. "But I wanted to meet the woman who finally captured Josh." His grin showed two rows of perfect white teeth. The man was impossibly perfect. "I've never known him to go out with any woman more than a couple of times."

I didn't know what to say, so I just nodded.

"Anyway. Get her home, Deitz. I'll see you guys at the funeral?"

I wanted to groan. The Mitner assignment was becoming the job from Hell. I wasn't sure I'd survive another episode.

"See you tomorrow," Eddie said, clasping the other man's hand.

I felt James' eyes on me as I started out the door and I stopped, turning back. "Thanks for helping to save me."

He nodded. "It was my pleasure. Good night."

I couldn't identify the emotion behind the look he gave me. That was a rarity for me. Mr. James was a mystery man.

Eddie helped me into his truck and turned up the heat. After a couple of minutes, we both stopped shivering. Alone with Deitz at last, I turned to him. "Eddie, we have a problem."

He glanced my way. "Are you all right? Do you need to go to the hospital?"

I shook my head hard as tears flooded my eyes.

Panic flared as I remembered how terrified I'd been. "I don't need a hospital. I think I need a cop."

He frowned. "A cop? Why?"

"Because I didn't fall into the Mitner's pool tonight. I was shoved in. And the person who pushed me had a warning for us."

Eddie's face looked gray in the glow from passing headlights. "What kind of warning?"

"He said to keep our noses out of this, or things were going to go badly for us."

"Dang."

I nodded. "Yeah. I'm pretty sure that *going bad* thing's already started for me."

Eddie pulled up in front of my apartment building, and I hissed.

He scanned me a look. "What's wrong?"

I jerked my head toward the long, dark figure leaning against a dented little car looking judgmental. "Argh."

"Is that May-speak for something? Or are you reprising a role from the Pirates of the Caribbean?"

I sighed and unhooked my seatbelt as Eddie pulled up behind the small, dented car. "I wish."

Climbing down from the truck's high seat, I nearly fell as my foot slipped off the wide running board. A big hand shot out to grab my arm. My visitor helped me down to the ground and then stood there, scratching his thick cap of dark brown hair. "What in the world are you wearing?"

I looked up into a hypercritical pair of gray eyes and fought my instinctive tendency toward defensiveness. "I had an accident."

Eddie came around the truck, and the disapproving gaze swung to encompass him. "What happened?"

"She was atta..."

"I fell into a pool," I hurried to interrupt Eddie. The last thing I needed was for Eddie to spill the beans to Mr. Judgmental that I'd been attacked and threatened by a possible murderer. "I'm fine, in case you're wondering."

The critical gaze slid over the skin-tight velour and stopped at my feet, where a pair of the world's ugliest sandals sat repulsive and landlocked on my feet. "What in the name of all that's fashionable are those?"

"Fish-flops," I told him with a straight face. "They're all the rage."

"Yeah, I'd be in a rage if I was wearing them too." Mr. Judgmental shook his head. "Have you called Dad?"

I frowned, realizing I hadn't taken my phone with me to the job. I couldn't remember the last time a job had me so discombobulated. Probably never. "I left my phone at home. What's up?"

Instead of answering my question, he slid a disparaging gaze to Eddie. "Are you responsible for her current state?"

Eddie bristled. I could almost feel his caveman rising, Hulk-like, from under his skin. But, to his credit, he restrained himself, offering Argh his hand. "Eddie Deitz. And you are...?"

"This rude, overprotective oaf is my brother. Argh, be nice to Eddie. He's a friend of Josh Mitner's." I lifted my eyebrows, trying to beam a message to my brother to play along. When I'd taken the job at Exit Stage Left, I'd warned my family they might have to support me in a ruse once in a while. They hadn't been happy about it. But it had finally been decided that, in the grand scheme of things, that type of little white fib wouldn't rest too heavily on their souls.

Argh narrowed his gaze on Eddie. "I'm sorry for your loss." He didn't sound at all sorry.

Eddie nodded, dropping the hand my stupid brother had never taken. "Thanks."

We stood in a triangle for a long, uncomfortable minute, Argh staring at Eddie and Eddie staring back. I stood at the apex of the triangle, wishing I could sink into the concrete under my fish-flops.

Finally, I couldn't take it anymore. "Well...thanks for the ride home, Eddie."

Eddie didn't act as if he'd heard me. "Argh, huh? Strange name."

Argh had long ago given up explaining the nick-name. He just shrugged.

"Is that Argh as in parrot on the shoulder and

patch on the eye, or is that just what people say when they see you coming?"

Argh fake-laughed. "Funny. I've never heard that one before."

"Argh had chronic eye infections as a kid. He was always wearing an eyepatch, so we dubbed him Argh," I explained.

"It's true," Argh said, crossing densely muscled arms over a gym-crafted chest. "They actually dubbed me that. With a plastic laser sword."

I nodded.

"You have a...unique...family, don't you, May?"

It was my turn to shrug. They felt kind of normal weird to me. "Anyway..."

Eddie finally got the hint. "I'll pick you up for the funeral?"

I shook my head, pointing to the dented little car. "Argh brought my car back. I can drive."

Eddie eyed the car skeptically. "You sure that thing will hold together long enough to get you there?"

Argh drew himself up, his jaw stiffening.

I held up a hand. "Ease down, Superpatch," I told my brother. To Eddie, I said, "No offense, but you should never judge a book or a car by its cover. Betty and I would challenge you and your truck to a street race any day."

Argh nodded smugly. "I'd pay to watch that."

"Betty?"

I ran a loving hand over my bucket of rust and dents. "This is Betty. She was Argh's best gal before I inherited her." I gave my brother a fond smile. "He still takes good care of her for me."

Argh cocked his head, his gaze tightening. "Have we met before? You look familiar."

"See you tomorrow, May." Eddie was in his truck and accelerating down the street before I could even respond.

I frowned. "That was strange."

"Yeah. There's something about that guy I don't trust. How well do you know him?" Argh asked.

"Not well. Just that he was the friend of the deceased client I've been fake-mourning."

"Well, watch your step with him. I've seen him somewhere before, and I don't think it was in a good way."

To change the subject, I pointed to Betty. "Thanks for fixing her up for me."

"You're welcome. She's good as new. Just needed a few plugs and some fresh oil to drink."

"You need a ride home?"

"Not home, no. My car's at Dad's. We're bringing dinner back."

"I have to grab Shakes."

He nodded. "I'll wait here. And change your clothes. Especially those stupid fish shoes. The googly eyes are giving me the creeps."

7

Though it had been three years since Mom had passed, I still felt a twinge of sadness every time we pulled up to the pretty white bungalow in the center of a big lot of mature trees. The Lieutenant had preserved the yard just as Mom had liked it, keeping a small part of her alive in the vibrant flower beds and close-cut, weed-free lawn.

But the irony of a stay-at-home mom in a family of mostly cops dying at the relatively young age of fifty-five still astounded me.

"The smell of that food is making me crazy," Argh complained.

Shoving a curly ribbon of hair out of my eyes, I gathered up the bags. "This is a lot of food for three people."

He grabbed the small bag of egg rolls off the top

and shoved one into his mouth. "Haff dyou theen usth eat?"

I made a grab for the bag, but Argh jumped out of the car.

Shakes jumped out too and ran after him, barking happily as Argh ran in circles around the yard, laughing madly.

"You'd better save me one of those!" I yelled after him as I struggled to grab all the bags and my purse.

Argh stopped running and swallowed, commanding my dog to do his business.

Shakes squatted obediently, peeing like a girl on a random dandelion that had somehow escaped the Lieutenant's rigid schedule of weed and feed, and then took off for the front door.

I smiled, knowing Shakes was anxious to see the Lieutenant, who would pretend he didn't like the Pomeranian Devil while cuddling with him on his lap all evening and feeding him scraps when I wasn't looking.

"We're here!" Argh called out as we entered the brightly lit home. I stopped inside the door, inhaling the familiar scents of Lavender potpourri, my Mom's favorite, and lemon dusting spray. The worn but comfortable furniture was still arranged the way it had been when I was a kid, and the fireplace danced with soft light despite the heat outside.

The Lieutenant liked to sit in front of the fire,

contemplating life. He cranked the air conditioner to accommodate his guilty pleasure.

Dad was sitting in his usual chair in front of the fire, the golden flames dancing shadows across his handsome face. He looked up when we opened the door, scowling when Argh bellowed. "I'm right here; you don't need to rattle the windows."

With a sharp, happy bark, Shakes bounced into the living room and leaped into his lap.

"Hello, rodent," the Lieutenant said, even as his big hands moved to scratch the special spot behind Shakes' ears that made him squint his eyes with pleasure.

Argh grabbed the food from my hand and held it up. "We brought Golden Dragon."

"Szechuan chicken?" the Lieutenant asked.

"Of course."

I made another grab for the tiny bag of egg rolls. "Give me one of those, you Neanderthal."

He danced away, laughing maniacally. "Mine, mine, all mine."

I looked at Dad. He reached out as Argh tried to dance by, snagging the bag and handing it to me. "Stop teasing your sister."

I looked down at the single, sad egg roll in the bag. "You ate almost all of them."

"You said to save you one. I saved you one."

He headed into the kitchen. "Get napkins!" I called out. My brother was usually good about grabbing plates and silverware. He never remembered the napkins. I dropped onto the couch, slipping my flip-flops off and leaning gratefully against the sofa's soft back. "It feels good to get off my feet."

The Lieutenant lifted Shakes and settled him more comfortably in his lap. "Tough day at the office?" He grinned.

Everybody in my family was amused by my chosen profession. They thought it was strange. I actually thought it was strange too. But I was okay with it. "You could say that. Did you find out anything about that...erm...thing we talked about yesterday?"

"After dinner."

Argh came back into the room and I got up, grabbing the TV trays from the stand behind the couch. I settled one in front of each of us, and Argh handed out plates and utensils. No napkins.

With a long-suffering sigh, I headed into the kitchen to grab them. When I came back, Argh was telling the Lieutenant about Eddie Deitz. "I think I might have arrested him once."

Dad glanced my way. "I had the same impression. Then I remembered where I've met him before."

"Where?" Argh asked, spearing a chunk of beef from his plate.

"He's a PI."

Argh slapped his knee. "That's it. I caught him

snooping around the Jacobs murder last year and brought him in."

Dad nodded. "That wasn't the only time our Mr. Deitz was discovered someplace where he shouldn't have been."

Biting my tongue on a strange desire to defend Eddie, I gave them each a napkin and settled down to fill my plate. We chatted about my other siblings while we ate. They were both cops, but my sister was heading for a desk job as she entered the second trimester of her first pregnancy. Sasha would hate being behind a desk. I felt bad for her. But I was secretly glad to have her off the mean streets of Asheville while she was pregnant.

My other brother, Dash, had just passed his Detectives exam and was going to be insufferable.

Argh had been a Detective for a year, and I remembered how hard he'd been to take after he'd passed the exam.

Twenty minutes later, I sat back, feeling like I was going to explode. I'd been hungry and had eaten way too much.

Apparently, tiny cheesecakes were not enough to sustain a person through nearly drowning and then dealing with a bratty older brother for a couple of hours.

Shakes was happily snoring in the Lieutenant's lap, his little belly full of Szechuan Chicken and rice, when Argh left to go start his shift.

The Lieutenant didn't waste any time getting to the topic du jour.

"You need to stay out of that Mitner mess, Punkin."

In the middle of picking a stray piece of cabbage out of my teeth with a toothpick, I stopped, fixing all my attention on the Lieutenant. "What are you telling me?"

"I'm telling you to get as far away from that as you can."

"But I have to go to the funeral tomorrow."

"I'd advise against it." His words seemed to give me the option, but his tone and body language were more along the lines of giving an order.

"It's my job, Dad."

He just barely kept from curling his lip in derision. But I read it in his eyes nonetheless.

I placed the toothpick on my plate and leaned forward, holding his gaze with mine. "Don't denigrate what I do."

Like his tone, mine was a message. I'd long ago made the decision to go my own way in my career. Aside from occasional jokes at my expense, my family had mostly accepted it and respected my decision. But the few times someone had crossed the line, I'd made sure they understood the decision was not up for discussion.

Knowing my family, I knew it had to be done.

Boundaries had to be set. Respect had to be earned. I was sticking to my guns.

He held my gaze for a beat and then lifted a hand, palm out. "Don't get your knickers in a twist, Punkin. I'm not dissing your job. I'm just saying that maybe, this one time, it's not worth getting hurt or... worse...over."

My brows climbed into my hairline. "You really believe I'm in danger?"

He smoothed a big hand over Shakes, clearly looking for the right words. "I believe...you've already been in danger from this situation."

How the heck did he know? "Who told you that?"

"Argh isn't as stupid as you'd like to believe."

I sighed. No. Argh wasn't stupid at all. In fact, his instincts as a cop were spot on. "Look, Dad, nothing's going to happen to me at the funeral tomorrow. I'll be surrounded by people. Once it's over, I'll walk away and never be involved again. I'll be fine."

"You'll walk away?"

"Scouts honor."

His lips curved up in a crooked grin. "You were never a scout, Punkin."

"I would have been if they'd let me go with the boys."

"The boy scouts weren't taking girls at that time, and you know it." The grin widened. "You were born too early. I believe they're taking girls now."

I frowned. "Figures."

He chuckled softly. Shakes looked up at him, adoration making his brown gaze go soft. I wanted to barf. "What is this magic that you weave over my dog?"

The Lieutenant ran his big fingers over Shakes' tiny head, his own gaze soft enough to horrify him if he could see himself. "I let him know I'm the boss. Dogs respect that." Shakes went belly up, his tail smacking the back of the chair. The Lieutenant dutifully scratched his fuzzy tummy.

"Yeah, I can see you're definitely in charge."

We sat in companionable silence for a few minutes. I glanced at the clock, weariness creeping in to knock me on my butt. But I couldn't leave yet. I had to try to pry information about Josh's death out of my dad. It wasn't going to be easy. Just as I demanded his respect for what I chose to do with my life, I had to respect his responsibilities as a cop.

One of those responsibilities was keeping police business to himself.

Still...

"Was Josh Mitner killed?"

The Lieutenant continued to scratch Shakes' wriggling tummy. He was silent for so long I thought he wasn't going to answer me. But finally, he looked up. "All I can tell you is that the truck which struck him didn't belong to any known trash companies. We have no idea where it came from or why it was there. Add to that the fact that Josh Mitner received a call five minutes before he was struck from an untraceable phone. Strange in and of itself, but explainable if there weren't other factors involved."

I leaned forward, intrigued. "What other factors?"

"When the accident hit the news, the 9-1-1 dispatcher received a call from someone who'd driven past an unmarked trash truck near the intersection moments before the crash occurred. The witness noticed the truck because it was sitting there, idling, with its lights off."

"That's strange."

"Yes, Punkin. That's strange enough to bring the little hairs on the back of my neck up. You know what happens when the little hairs on the back of my neck stand up, right?"

I sighed. "You investigate."

"Yes, May. I investigate. And that's exactly what I'm going to do. And I don't need you or your private investigator friend, Deitz, getting in my way."

"Deitz told me he's a PI," I said. "Is he any good?"

"Actually, yes, he is. Except that he has a tendency to stick his nose in where it doesn't belong. This is police business, and I don't want him mucking up my investigation."

My dad's words made me shudder. They were too close to the whispered warning beside the pool. "So, you and Deitz have met before?" I really wanted his opinion about Eddie Deitz, but I was afraid to ask for fear he'd think I was interested in the guy.

"Yep. I arrested him for impeding an investigation. Twice. Now that was a while ago. But I'm not stupid enough to think he's cleaned up his act. I figure he's just gotten better at hiding his activities. I don't want you involved in those activities, MayBell."

"I can't control what he does."

"No. And I'll deal with him. But you *can* control what *you* do. And that's what I'm telling you to do."

8

Just my luck, the drought would finally break when I was on a job and had to be outside. I stood under the biggest black umbrella I could find and tried to focus on the words being spoken by the pastor.

My gaze kept wandering around the assembled crowd. Seeing all the faces, some familiar and some not, prickles of unease crept down my back on sharp little feet. The person who'd shoved me into the pool might be there, standing mere feet away. He might have even been invited to the wake rather than crashing it as I'd originally assumed.

I blinked, wondering if there was a way to get hold of that invitation list. Would the Mitners have been that organized? Maybe they'd just told everybody when and where it would be as they had with me and let people come and go at will.

There was only one way to find out.

I mentally kicked myself. I was doing exactly what the Lieutenant had told me not to do. That was the moment I realized, with a fair amount of consternation, that my dad knew me better than I knew myself. He'd known I'd be unable to resist sticking my nose into the case.

Even the fact that I was calling it a case showed I was already involved in it.

In *the case*.

I winced. I was hopeless.

Beside me, Mrs. Mitner stood dry-eyed. Her gaze was slightly glassy, and I assumed she'd been drugged into calmness. I had a sudden urge to wrap an arm around her. If it had been my mom standing there, I'd have wanted someone to give her comfort.

My gaze slipped to Alex Mitner. He had more color in his cheeks than he'd had the night before, and his eyes were dry. But his gaze was skimming the crowd just as I'd been doing. I wondered if he was thinking the killer might be there too.

"Amen," said the pastor.

"Amen," said the crowd.

I blinked in surprise as Mrs. Mitner stepped forward, her husband finally taking her arm and helping her to the casket, where she laid a single, long-stemmed white rose on the shiny surface.

The Mitner's walked away, heading for the dark

SUV waiting at the curb. Mr. Mitner was all but holding his wife up as she stumbled toward the car.

"Are you okay?"

I looked up into Eddie's eyes and nodded. "I feel so badly for her."

He looked at me strangely. "Family and friends are going to the house. I don't suppose you're interested?"

I started to shake my head and then remembered I wanted to ask about the guest list from the night before. "I don't want to, but I do need to return Mrs. Mitner's clothes to her."

I'd washed and dried the velour suit early that morning. I hadn't bothered washing the fish flops. I figured a little masking dirt might improve rather than take away from their inherent ugliness.

"Do you mind if I ride along? My car's at the house. I rode over with the Mitners."

I nodded, and he took my arm as we began to pick our way over the soggy grass. My umbrella kept hitting him in the cheek, so he took it from me and held it over both of us.

"I spoke to the Lieutenant last night."

Eddie spared me a quick, suspicious glance. "Oh?"

"Yeah. He remembered where he'd met you before."

Deitz sighed. "I hope you're not going to hold it against me?"

I shrugged. "I get being passionate about your job. But he's already warned me to stay away from all this." I swung an arm to encompass the cemetery and the guests hurrying to their cars.

"From cemeteries? Funerals?"

I gave him a look and dug my keys out of my black clutch. "You know what I mean."

He took the keys and opened my door for me, holding the umbrella over my head as I ducked inside.

When he was in the passenger seat, I glanced his way. "It's hard always being surrounded by cops."

"I can imagine." He frowned. "What do they think about you being an actress?"

"Actor."

His lips twitched. "Sorry. How sexist of me."

I shrugged. "It's not that. I just don't think women should be named or treated differently for doing the same job. We don't call female cops copess'."

He chuckled. "Good point. But you didn't answer my question."

"I think they mostly respect me for going my own way. But deep down, I suspect they believe what I do isn't important."

"If it's any consolation, I think it is."

I didn't even try to hide my shock. "You do?"

"Yep. Entertaining people is important. People need books, theater, and music. It's an important part of our lives. It keeps us sane in a crazy, confusing world."

Against my will, my lips curved upward. "I couldn't agree more."

His dark brows lowered, and his face darkened. Warning bells went off in my brain. "But what *you* do is different, isn't it? No less important, I guess. But different. You pretend to be someone you're not when people are at their most vulnerable. It rides a razor edge between being a good thing and a bad thing."

Heat flooded my face. I knew that if I looked in the mirror, my cheeks would be fiery red. "What are you trying to say, Deitz?"

He held my gaze, not backing down a smidge. "I'm saying I know you're a fake mourner at a company called Exit Stage Left. Clever name. I'm sure your clients get quite a chuckle out of it."

My hands tightened on the steering wheel. "Now you're just being mean."

"Am I?" He leaned close, his nose mere inches from mine, and his face was flushed too. "Josh was my best friend. He was murdered in the prime of his life. And you stand around pretending to know him? Lying to everyone about it? Pretending you understand their pain?"

I didn't back away. "I do understand their pain. I've lived it. Recently. Myself. I'm not lying. I'm doing a job that I was hired to do. And I'd like to think I've given people comfort from my work."

We glared at each other for a long moment. Then Eddie seemed to deflate, some of the angry color leaving his face. He sat back, scrubbing a hand over his eyes. "I know about your mom."

I gasped. "What the heck? Did you do background on me?"

"I did. I'm sure your dad told you what I do for a living. I needed to know who you really were."

"Why is it so hard for you to believe I could have been Josh's girlfriend?"

"Because Josh didn't have girlfriends. He was a free agent and happy to be one. And because if you'd dated Josh, your name would have been Cherry or Bambi or something equally clichéd."

I blinked. "Oh."

"Yeah. Josh had a type. And let's just say you're the opposite of that type."

"Got it." I sat back, my chest heaving with emotion. "The Mitners hired me. It won't do you any good to out me to them."

He shook his head. "That's not what this is about."

"Then what?"

"I don't like being lied to."

I lifted my hands. "Hello? You haven't exactly told me your life's story. I think we've both been guilty of some level of dishonesty. At least I had a legitimate excuse."

He frowned. "You have a point. As much as it galls me."

Despite myself, I smiled.

He caught me grinning and barked out a laugh. "Okay, let's start over." He held out his hand. "Eddie Deitz, PI and friend of the deceased. I'm pretty sure Josh was murdered. I intend to find out who killed him."

I nodded, taking his hand. "MayBell Ferth, mourning actor at Exit Stage Left. And, after being threatened and nearly killed last night, I'm inclined to agree with you that Josh was murdered."

"Good. We'll start there." He fixed me with an intense gaze. "Do you want to help me find out who killed Josh?"

My heart said yes as my head shook no. "I shouldn't."

"I know your dad warned you away from this but, to be honest, May, I'm pretty sure you're safer if you stick close to me. Whoever killed Josh has clearly decided that you and I are a danger to them."

Horror made my stomach twist as I realized he was right. "Still..."

"I won't pressure you. But if you change your mind..."

"I'll let you know." I started the car and pulled away from the curb. In the moments since we'd climbed into Betty, the cemetery had emptied. We were one of only two cars still there.

The other one was a black SUV that looked a lot like the Mitners'.

As I wound my way through *Riverside Cemetery,* a question occurred to me. "Why do you supposed Mr. Mitner felt the need to hire me to play Josh's girlfriend?"

Deitz clipped his seatbelt and sat back, sighing. "He thought Josh was gay, and it embarrassed him."

"That's so sad..."

There was a horrendous crunching sound. Betty jerked forward, falling off the narrow cemetery road and bouncing along the grass.

We missed a big, granite monument by inches and were heading for another one. With a panicked cry, I yanked the wheel to the left and managed to miss the headstone, sideswiping a memorial vase and sending flower petals flying.

I fought the car as we bounced over a fresh grave and finally managed to ease her back onto the road. When we were moving smoothly forward again, I pulled air into my lungs. "What just happened? I thought we'd blown a tire, but clearly that wasn't it."

Eddie was turned in his seat, his wide gaze focused through the back window. "I'm afraid not. It appears your friend from last night isn't going to wait to see if we accepted his warning."

I glanced in the rear-view mirror just in time to see the big, dark car accelerate toward us again.

"Oh no, you don't!" I hit the gas and Betty shot forward, sending Eddie slamming back into his seat with the power of her acceleration. "Hold on, Deitz. This is gonna get bumpy."

The SUV hung back for a beat, probably surprised by the velocity with which my car had moved. But it didn't take the driver long to adjust. A beat later, the car was surging toward us again.

I watched it come, my gaze wavering between the mirror and the narrow winding road ahead. I eyed the distance to the exit, wondering if we could make it out onto open road, where we might get lucky and be seen speeding along by a patrol cop.

But that didn't seem likely. There was a lot of narrow, winding road between us and the large iron gates. Encompassing over eighty-seven acres and overlooking the *French Broad River, Riverside Ceme-*

tery was one of Asheville's largest and oldest cemeteries. Josh's family had a section clear at the back, in
a beautiful but secluded section of the cemetery.

The SUV surged forward. I pressed a little
harder on the gas, conscious of the hairpin turn
coming up an eighth of a mile ahead. As the car
neared my bumper, I jerked the wheel sideways,
easing off the road and shooting between a crypt
and a double monument with inches to spare.

We blasted past a concrete angel and I said a
quick prayer, hoping she was open for business as
the SUV kept pace with us on the nearby road.

I jerked Betty right and then left and right again,
easing her around monuments and under the over-
arching branches of a big tree on a small hill.

Her tires left the ground for a beat as we came
over the top of the hill, and I saw with chagrin that
we were headed for another crypt. I couldn't steer
around it with my tires off the ground. Betty's front
tires hit the grass. I jerked the wheel hard. We
careened toward the big memorial, grass and flowers
flying up behind us as Betty's rear tires skimmed
over a gravesite and skidded under the violence of
the turn.

We skipped sideways a couple of feet, the granite
walls of the crypt flying up on us as Betty fought to
gain purchase on the slippery, wet grass. We missed
the crypt by mere inches, shooting forward to ease
past another tree and between two more gravesites.

Ahead of us was a narrow ribbon of flat markers, with only the memorial vases filled with colorful plastic flowers to show where the gravesites were. Obstacles were light in that section, but there were fewer places to hide too.

I slammed on the brakes, and we skidded to a stop mere inches from the first marker.

To our right, the SUV eased to a stop, idling quietly as a soft rain sifted down onto its glossy surface. Its darkened windows hid the driver from sight. Without a human face to blame for its aggressiveness, the car itself felt like something evil stalking poor Betty.

Eddie and I stared at the big SUV. My heart pounded, and I was huffing air as if I'd just run a marathon.

"What now?" I asked the PI next to me.

He shook his head. "Can you outrun it?"

I slid my gaze over the field in front of us. "On the open road, no problem. But trying to avoid driving over these gravesites, in slippery grass, I'm not sure."

He nodded, pulling out his phone and handing it to me. "Call your brother."

I bit my lip. The last thing I wanted to do was involve my family.

Eddie lifted dark brows in question. "Do you want *me* to call him?"

"No. I don't want either of us to call him. I want

to figure out how to get out of this without involving my family."

"Fair enough," Eddie said. "But that means outrunning the SUV over those gravesites."

I expelled air, working my bottom lip as I ran through my options. I looked in the rearview mirror, trying to see an option back there I'd missed. The germ of an idea occurred. I looked left. A lone car eased along the road leading to the back of the cemetery.

I made my decision.

I slipped Betty into reverse. "Hold on!" I hit the gas, shooting backward with my gaze locked on the rearview mirror. A few feet away from a monument, I slammed on the brakes and shoved it into *Drive*, jamming my foot down on the gas again. We shot forward, staying in the narrow aisle between the top of one row of headstones and the bottom of the other.

"Where are you going?" Eddie screamed over Betty's roaring engine.

"There's an exit back here that not too many people know about." I pressed the brakes as Betty's tires hit the loose dirt of a freshly dug grave and slid sideways. We hit the corner of a flat marker and the tires found purchase, allowing us to shoot forward again. "What's the SUV doing?"

"He's barreling around on the road. I think he's planning on cutting us off."

Panic flared in my breast. He'd be able to make better time than Betty on the nice smooth road. But at the same time, he had to slow for turns and at least one curve. With our straight trajectory, I was hoping I had enough of a head start to give us an edge.

It was going to be close.

Dangerously close.

I pressed harder on the gas, my arms starting to ache from the constant corrections on the uneven ground.

The road I needed was just ahead. I shot a look toward the SUV and saw that he'd made great time. He was about two city blocks away and closing fast.

I gave Betty gas and she shimmied a bit, her tires bouncing mercilessly over the wet grass. The road shot up fast and, when Betty's tires were five feet away, I hit the brakes and turned the wheel. Betty's back end spun around and I corrected, sending us into a sideways slide that slowed when all four tires hit the pavement.

I didn't wait for the slide to stop. I hit the gas and shot forward, my eye on a caretaker's hut about fifty yards ahead and on the right. If I remembered right, there was a short gravel drive leading to the hut.

I'd be forced to slow for that.

"Where is it?" I shouted to Eddie.

"Twenty yards and closing fast."

"Dang!" Betty gave a throaty roar as I pressed her

pedal to the floor, earning us a few much-needed yards as the gravel drive came into sight.

"I'm going to have to make this interesting. I don't want him to know what I'm doing until it's too late for him to follow."

Eddie barked out a laugh. "This hasn't been interesting so far?"

I spared him a grin. "Saddle up, cowboy."

We were fifteen feet from the drive when I slammed on the brakes. Betty's back tires squealed and sent up a cloud of black smoke. She fishtailed for a beat before I eased up on the brake and, as the gravel road shot up on our right, yanked the wheel to send Betty's front end onto the rocks.

Behind us, the SUV hit the brakes, the big tires striking a puddle and sending water in a spray that accompanied a truly impressive fish-tail. The slide carried the top-heavy car's back end off the road. It crunched into a sapling before the driver overcorrected and sent the front tires off a wedge monument, careening into the air.

I didn't wait to see how he landed. I accelerated toward the hut, my eyes fixed on a spot just behind it.

Eddie braced his hands on the dash and jammed his feet into the floorboards. "May!"

I almost grinned. At the last possible moment, I turned the wheel and swerved around the small hut, heading down a rutted dirt road toward an opening between two massive trees.

A moment later, we were speeding along a tree-lined road, clear pavement behind us as far as the eye could see.

I parked in front of the Mitners' and we climbed out. We stood on the wet asphalt for a moment, letting the excitement of the cemetery chase ease away before we went inside.

Eddie caressed Betty's panting front end, shaking his head. "I don't know which one of you girls I want to propose to first."

I snickered. "Betty's easier to live with. I snore and hog the bed."

Eddie's dark brows climbed skyward. "You don't say."

I flushed with embarrassment. "Awkward."

He chuckled. "That was some pretty fantastic driving back there."

I couldn't stop a pleased grin from forming. "The Lieutenant made us all train in Advanced Precision Driving at the police testing facility. I excelled in skid control."

"I'll say you did." Eddie's gaze found mine, and I saw new respect there. "If I ever decide to take up a life of crime, will you be my getaway driver?"

I shook my head. "Not a chance. I might be good at skid turns, but nobody beats Argh for high-speed pursuit."

"Okay, no life of crime for me." Eddie leaned against Betty, crossing his arms over his chest. "I'm worried about you staying alone."

If I was honest, I worried about that too. "I'll be fine. I have Shakes."

His derisive snort carried me to the razor edge of my temper. "You aren't dissing my dog, are you?"

"May, he weighs ten pounds on a good day. His nose is barely bigger than my thumb. A good-sized rat could take him down without even working too hard."

I nodded, leaning a hip against my car. Reaching down, I laid my hand on her still-warm hood. "You misjudged Betty."

Eddie opened his mouth to argue and then thought better of it. "You're right. I did."

"You've been undervaluing me."

"I'm ashamed to say that I have. But that will never happen again."

"Yet you're going to underestimate my dog?"

He sighed. "Okay. I'll keep an open mind. But I'd still feel better if Shakes weighed a hundred and ten pounds more and had a jaw that could crunch something bigger than my pinky."

"Point taken. But I know how to take care of myself."

Eddie lifted his hands. "I give up. You are woman, hear you roar." He glanced toward the Mitner home, which seemed much quieter than it had the night before. I wondered if everybody had already gone home. "What did you *really* want from the Mitners?" he asked.

"You didn't buy my returning the clothes story?"

"No. Although I can see why you'd want to get those carp clogs out of your house as quickly as possible."

"Fish flops. And yes, that was a motivating factor. But I was thinking, whoever pushed me into the pool last night had most likely been a guest at the wake."

Eddie frowned. "I was thinking he'd snuck in just to give us a warning, but you might be right. It's not implausible to think that the person who killed Josh knew the family."

"I wondered if Mrs. Mitner was just organized enough to have had a guest list."

"I like the way you think. Okay. You ditch the shark shoes, distracting Mrs. M at the same time, and I'll sneak into the office and see if I can find a list."

A woman in a maid's uniform opened the door to us and stared blankly when I asked to speak to Mrs. Mitner.

Eddie slipped away as I was trying to talk my way past the blank look. I quickly learned the woman spoke very little English. Her accent sounded like French to my professionally trained ear. That possibility was just too clichéd for me. But then she wasn't hanging out of a too-tight uniform, so I assumed she was the real thing.

The pretty young maid finally pointed toward the stairs. "Mrs.," she said with a charming lisp.

I quickly jogged up the stairs, my head on a swivel to make sure I wasn't seen. I didn't know why I was on the lookout, but I had a burning need to just do what I came to do and get the heck out of there. My recent experiences in the Mitner home hadn't been great.

I reached the top of the steps and stood looking around. A balcony ran all the way around the top floor. It was open to the large entryway below except for a beautiful, curved railing. The hallway sported way too many doors. Some I presumed were closets. One was most likely a bathroom. But I figured there were at least six bedrooms to search.

I expelled a weary breath. Nothing was ever easy.

I found Valerie Mitner behind the third door I

opened. Actually, the door was already ajar. When I clasped the knob, it pushed into the room.

She was sitting so still my mind didn't register that it was her at first. I saw the slender woman, back ramrod straight, sitting on the edge of the big bed across the room, staring toward an open closet door. A few articles of clothing hung from hangers, some of them crooked and tangled on the rod. But most of the clothing appeared to be missing from the closet.

I looked around the room, seeing the discarded clothing strewn over furniture, taking note of the disheveled bed and the posters decorating the walls. It was a masculine room. And judging by the posters of bikini-clad women, a young man's room.

Josh's room.

"Mrs. Mitner?" I said softly so as not to startle her.

She didn't move. Didn't acknowledge me in any way. I waited a beat and tried again. "Mrs. Mitner, I brought your clothes back."

Nothing.

I moved into the room, wading through piles of shirts and jeans and a wide variety of shoes to get to the grieving mother. As I rounded the end of the bed, I jerked to a stop. She was still staring into the closet, her expression filled with rage rather than sadness, and she clutched the tattered remains of a tee shirt in one hand and a pair of scissors in the other. Between her feet on the floor was a pile of chopped-up fabric.

Mrs. Mitner was slicing and dicing her dead son's clothes.

"Um, Mrs. Mitner, are you okay?" I spoke softly, my gaze darting from her face to the scissors in her hand.

She was clutching them so hard her knuckles were white.

"Mrs. Mitner?"

She blinked and finally looked up at me, frowning. "What are you doing here?"

I held up the bag of clothes and shoes. "I brought your clothes back." Valerie Mitner looked at the bag as if she had no idea what I was talking about. After a moment, I tried again. "I see you're cleaning out some of Josh's things. Do..." I swallowed hard, not sure if it was my place to step in. But the woman was so obviously struggling. "Would you like me to help box them up?"

She looked at the scissors and the remains of the tee-shirt and opened her hand, letting the fabric fall to the floor. She lifted the scissors and stared at them.

I had a sudden, horrifying vision of her stabbing them into her own chest.

"Why don't you let me take those." I reached out slowly, easing my hand toward hers while keeping an eye on her expression. My fingers finally clasped the scissors and, with a gentle tug, I was able to pull them from her grip.

As soon as they were gone, she seemed to collapse, her narrow shoulders rounding. "I hate him for leaving me."

I closed my eyes. There it was. She'd moved from sadness to anger in the grieving process.

I settled the scissors onto a nearby tall dresser and put the bag of clothes I'd brought back next to them. Then I sat down on the bed and wrapped an arm around Josh's mom. I took a deep breath and shared something that I hadn't shared with many people. "I lost my mother a couple of years ago. I wouldn't even say her name for six months. Every time someone tried to talk to me about her, I shut them down. It does get easier in time. But nothing will ever completely fill that hole in your heart."

She shuddered violently and then laid her head on my shoulder. "Thank you for not lying to me. Everybody keeps telling me that it will get better. My brain knows that's probably true, but my heart is breaking. The last thing I want to hear is that someday I'll forget him."

"No. You'll never forget him. But the pain will ease, and you'll eventually be able to remember the good things without your lungs locking up."

She nodded, sniffling. Silvery tears slipped down her cheeks and landed on her hands, which were folded in her lap. "Why did they do this to me?"

My spidey senses perked up. "Who?"

"Why did it have to be Josh? It should have been Alex."

Hooboy! "Mrs. Mitner, are you saying Josh was killed because of something your husband did?"

She didn't answer me for a long moment. I bit my lip, unsure whether I should press.

"He never understood our son. Josh was gentle and sweet. But he was unserious. He had no ambitions other than to have the next good time." She shook her head, straightening up and blowing her nose on a tissue she pulled from the pocket of her sweater. "He wouldn't have hurt anyone. Joshua saw what his father had become and didn't want that for himself. Alex could never forgive him for that."

"What had his father become?"

She expelled a weary sigh. "Look what a mess I've made of things."

I realized she wasn't going to expound on what she'd said, and I didn't have the heart to press. She was in so much pain. "How about I help you clean it up. Between the two of us, it won't take any time at all."

She nodded. "Thank you, May."

When I came back downstairs an hour later, carting a big box of Josh's clothes, Eddie was nowhere to be seen. I placed the box next to the front door as instructed and went in search of him. I found him sitting in Alex Mitner's study, drinking something amber-colored from a cut-glass tumbler.

Alex was sitting behind his desk with a matching glass. Only his was empty. He looked up when I knocked on the door frame. "May. Come in. Would you like a scotch?"

I nodded. "Thanks."

He poured two fingers and handed it to me. I sat down in the chair next to Eddie. "This is a great room. So genuine and peaceful."

Alex nodded, looking around as if seeing it for the first time. "I come here when I need to think."

The hardwood floors shone under dense, black oriental rugs. The walls were covered in what looked like taupe-colored leather. The industrial metal desk was an anchor in the center of the main space. An oversized fireplace was the focus of a small sitting room to the side, situated between two sets of French doors. A fire danced behind a glass screen in the fireplace, the cozy light making happy shadows on the overstuffed club chairs in front of it.

Heavy, black draperies were pulled back from the French doors overlooking the pool. I could see the massive skeleton of the tree that had trapped me. It was still sprawled across the formerly tidy patio.

"We need to get that cut up and carted away," Alex said as he saw me staring at it. He narrowed his gaze. "Are you okay?"

I nodded. "I won't lie. It scared the stuffing out of me. But it all turned out okay."

"Thanks to Eddie here and James." Alex shook his head. "I appreciate you not making a stink about it."

I shrugged. "It was an accident." I took a sip of the scotch and nearly sighed as it slid warm and happy down my throat, exploding into pleasant heat in my belly. I couldn't believe I was drinking so early in the day.

Alex held his newly refilled glass, rolling it from side to side between his hands, but he didn't seem to be drinking it. He looked far away. Sad.

There was an awkward silence which I felt compelled to fill. "Your wife and I packed up some of Josh's things."

He lifted his brows. "Oh? It seems soon."

"It is. But everybody grieves in their own way. Mrs. Mitner seems to need it right now." I didn't tell him about the scissors or the trash bag full of severed clothing I'd carried down to the kitchen and hidden among the bags of refuse gathered from the wake. I'd slipped the scissors into that bag, just in case Mrs. Mitner got inspired to grab them again.

"She might need to talk to someone," I said carefully. "A therapist."

I expected him to get hostile or argue. But after an initial surprised arch of his eyebrows, he sighed, nodding. "I know. I'll get her in first thing tomorrow."

"Good." I glanced at Eddie. He was still staring at the glass in his hands. I wondered what had happened before I'd come down. I'd planned to talk to Deitz about what Mrs. Mitner had said. He'd known the family a while and could probably shed some light on her strange half-statements.

But given the situation and the opportunity, I decided to just plunge in. "Your wife seems to think Josh was killed because of something you were involved in. Do you know why she'd think that?"

Eddie's head jerked up and he gave me a look I couldn't decipher.

I got the impression I'd made a mistake, but I couldn't take it back.

Eddie and Alex shared a glance.

"I'm sorry if that question was out of line," I told Alex. "But that's what your wife is thinking. I thought you'd want to know."

He drained the crystal tumbler he'd just refilled and slammed it down on the desktop.

I winced.

"Everybody wants to blame me for this."

"Alex," Eddie said in a warning tone as he sat up straighter in his chair. "Don't kill the messenger."

Mr. Mitner scrubbed a meaty hand over his face. "You're right. I'm sorry, May. That *is* important to know. I'll talk to her."

The cop genes engaged my mouth before the civilian genes could stop them. "Is there a good reason why she'd feel that way?"

Mitner spun his glass on the desk blotter, his expression sad. "I'm sure you can understand, with the business I'm in, people assume certain things about you."

I cast my memory back to the dossier I'd received on Josh and his family. They owned *Mitner's Crime Clean*, the largest and most successful post-trauma cleanup service in the country. Probably the world. Alex Mitner had offices in every major city in the US. He was a very wealthy man, with access to a very specific set of skills and knowledge that I assumed lots of unsavory people might crave. "You work closely with the police?"

His gaze shot up, fixing intently on me. "Sometimes. But ideally, the crime scene techs have already gotten what they needed by the time we're called in."

"Ideally? Not always?"

"Cops are like everybody else. They're not all good at what they do. We've been known to uncover an errant cartridge, needle, or suspicious liquid they'd missed. Our record with the police is solid. We have protocols in place to address everything. When we find something that might be pertinent to creating a strong case against a criminal, we immediately stop work and contact the officer in charge."

I nodded and let a moment skim by before I

asked him another question. "Have you ever gotten pressure to 'overlook' something?"

He narrowed his gaze. "Did you miss the part where I said we come in *after* the police?"

"No. But as you said, not all police officers are good at their jobs. In fact, some don't even try to be good. If you know what I mean."

Eddie apparently couldn't keep quiet any longer. "Are you talking about dirty cops?"

I shrugged. "It happens, unfortunately."

"It probably does," Alex agreed. "But I've never been asked to overlook evidence. My *Crime Clean* business is well-respected. My reputation is pristine. I have to say I resent your implications."

"I'm sorry, Mr. Mitner. But if Josh was killed because of something you did or didn't do, it makes sense, given your profession, as you pointed out, that it might have something to do with *Crime Clean*. I'm just trying to help find Josh's killer."

He screwed up his face. "You do know I only hired you to mourn at my son's funeral, right? You're not a private investigator."

"No. I'm not a PI." I swung a glance toward Eddie, who other than clarifying my earlier point, had been suspiciously quiet. "But I come from a family of cops, and I'm afraid I'm used to asking a lot of questions when something doesn't add up."

Mitner glared across his desk. "Josh's death was

an accident. No questions are necessary. This is none of your concern."

He seemed to have forgotten asking Eddie to get to the bottom of Josh's death when I'd been standing there.

Alex pushed to his feet, his glower softening only a smidge. "Thank you for doing your job through all the drama. You've gone over and above. I'll be sure to tell your employer."

I knew a dismissal when I heard one. Reluctantly, I stood. "Thank you for the feedback, Mr. Mitner." After one last glance at Eddie, who seemed to have slumped deeper into his chair and had the nearly empty tumbler attached to his lower lip, I left.

I was still mad twenty minutes later when I arrived home.

My mood hadn't been improved by the sight of the fish-flops on Betty's passenger side floor. Apparently, they were a "gift" from Mrs. Mitner.

10

My doorbell rang as I was drying my hair while going over the dossier for my upcoming assignment. I didn't hear it over the dryer, but Shakes jumped up from where he'd been curled on my damp towel, cocking his head at me in question.

Preoccupied with my thoughts, his sudden movement didn't immediately register.

Despite my attempts to research my upcoming role, my mind kept wandering to Josh Mitner and his unfortunate and untimely death.

More specifically, I couldn't help thinking about the absurdity of my being tangled in his murder like pepperoni in an extra cheese pizza.

Shakes started to bark. I yelled at him to shush.

He quieted for a beat but then started up again.

When he took off running toward the front door,

I finally turned off the hairdryer, just in time to hear the bell ring again. By the time I pulled open the door, Eddie was facing off with the pothead next door.

"Dude!"

I waved at my neighbor. "Hey, Doug."

Shakes trotted out into the hallway and barked happily at Doug, his tail wagging.

Eyeing my little dog with suspicion, my neighbor shifted from one long, bare foot to the other, and a smoky scent wafted my way. It was almost enough to give me a second-hand high. "I'm tryin' to concentrate on my shows."

"Sorry. I'll try to answer my door faster next time."

Doug nodded, dipping his weak, bristly chin to Eddie. "Dude."

Eddie gave him a jaunty, sideways wave and Doug retreated back into his smoky abode.

Shakes bounced around Eddie's feet, whining until Deitz picked him up and succumbed to the appropriate number of chin kisses. "Hey, buddy."

I leaned against the door frame. "Did I know you were coming?"

Eddie cast a look over my white wife-beater and puppy print boxers. "I hope not."

Rolling my eyes, I stepped backward. "Come on in before you disrupt Doug and his shows again."

"Is there a new season of *Naked and Stoned* I should know about?"

I chuckled. "Would you like something to drink?"

"I'd love a beer."

I opened my refrigerator and pulled out one beer and one diet soda. Handing him the beer, I popped the tab on the soda can and sipped gratefully. "I'm surprised to see you again."

Eddie moved over to my couch and plopped down onto it, resting the beer on one thigh and his dark head on the back of my sofa. "I didn't like the way we left things."

Shakes jumped up and circled next to him, curling up with a contented sigh.

"Oh? I'm not sure why. You didn't say anything insulting or rude. In fact, you didn't say much of anything at all."

He lifted his head and looked at me. "Sorry. It was just...sitting there talking about Josh was depressing. I guess it just hit me how much I'm going to miss him."

"I totally get that." I lowered myself onto the other end of the couch and sat cross-legged, leaning back and sipping from the icy can.

Eddie absently petted Shakes, his expression thoughtful. "Your questions were good ones."

"Huh?"

"To Alex. Those were all questions I'd have asked him if I could."

"Why couldn't you?"

Eddie sipped his beer. "I just can't."

I did a mental shrug and changed the subject. Eddie would tell me what was bothering him when he was ready. In the meantime, I had more questions. "Did you get the guest list?"

"I did. I haven't had a chance to go over it in detail yet. But at first glance, I didn't see anybody who seemed even remotely questionable. All except for the doc and James are close friends or family."

"What's the deal with James?"

He gave me a suspicious look. "Why?"

"I just wondered how he fit into the mix. You excluded him from both close friends and family."

"Oh. James went to school with Josh and me. He's a good guy. A little too driven at times. Comes from a really poor family and built himself a successful business fairly quickly. I think he's been working with Alex on some project."

"At *Crime Clean*?"

"Not sure. I haven't had a one-on-one with James for a while."

"Is there any chance he's our killer?"

"Not unless Josh tried to steal his girl," Eddie joked. As soon as he made the joke, he paled, looking spooked. "Oh."

"Okay, that's clearly something we need to rule out."

"Yeah. We should. But I really don't believe James would 'gack' Josh for sleeping with a woman. Neither one of them is that into monogamy."

"Still."

"Yeah. I'll propose dinner or something and pick his brain."

"Good. And you already know I'm suspicious about the doctor."

"Yeah. That one's going to be a bit harder. He's not a real open guy. I don't even know his first name."

"Is he Alex's personal physician?"

"No. Actually, he's a forensic pathologist. He used to work for the Medical Examiner's office. Now he consults on *Crime Clean* and Alex's secondary, private autopsy business."

I lifted my eyebrows. "Curiouser and curiouser. You realize that makes my theory that Josh's murder was tied to something at *Crime Clean* even stronger, right?"

Eddie didn't respond at first.

"Hello?"

He looked up and I was shocked to see guilt in his gaze. "I have something to confess."

My heart skipped a beat. *Please don't let him tell me he's the killer.* "Should I grab my mace?"

He didn't even crack a smile. "You know how I

told you that I've been focusing on a case for a new client?"

I nodded, dreading what he was about to tell me.

He sighed. "I didn't lie about that. Not exactly. But I left something really important out of it." When I frowned, he went on. "The client I was helping was Alex. Someone has been threatening him."

I stared at him for a long moment and then lowered my gaze, knowing he'd see the anger there. "You certainly waited long enough to tell me."

He gave me a look. "Are you going to pretend you've been entirely honest with me all this time?"

I chewed the inside of my lower lip. "You know everything there is to know about me."

"Because I did background. If I hadn't, would you have fessed up to lying about being Josh's girlfriend?"

"I wasn't lying. I was doing a job. You should understand that if anybody should. I'm sure you misrepresent yourself all the time in the pursuit of information."

"Okay, I'll give you that. Let's put the accusations aside and focus on the information we have."

I nodded. "Who was threatening Alex and why?"

"He claims he doesn't know."

"But you don't believe him?"

"He's lying."

"Then how in the world does he expect you to find out who it is?"

"To be honest, I don't think he does expect me to find out. I'm not even sure the person exists. I have a sneaking suspicion Alex was just trying to get me out of the way."

Curiouser and curiouser. "Why?"

"Because I pay attention. I notice things. Like, for example, I noticed that Alex met face to face with William Tomlinson a few weeks ago."

I frowned. "Why does that name sound familiar?"

"Maybe because he's a rich businessman who's considering running for Mayor. Or maybe because he's been accused of killing his girlfriend. Unfortunately, the evidence they have against him is all circumstantial. They need to find the weapon."

"I remember that murder. Wasn't it a couple of months ago?"

"Yeah. It's definitely a cooling case. And I'm pretty sure they won't find the weapon."

"Why not?"

"Because I believe Alex's cleaners took evidence from the scene. And I think Alex is holding onto that evidence for whatever reason. And I think there's a good chance it got Josh killed."

I sat there for a long moment, thinking about what he'd said. It was all new information, taking me in an entirely new direction, but it made a slimy kind of sense. "Okay, if what you say is true, why Josh? You don't think he was involved in the evidence tampering, do you?"

"No. Although, I'll admit there's an outside chance he was. Josh was a risk-taker. He got high from taking impossible chances. But he also hated his dad's occupation. And lately, I don't know if he was finally starting to grow up or what, but he seemed almost angry about the business. He'd begun to hate it and his father." Eddie shook his head.

"Like he'd learned something he didn't like?" I offered.

Eddie's gaze shot to mine. "Exactly like that."

"Okay, let's assume for the moment that Josh wasn't in on it. Would he have taken an active interest in changing it?"

"What do you mean?"

"I mean, would Josh have tried to *out* his father for the crime?"

"I'm not sure. But he definitely might have gotten proactive about finding out the details."

"Because...?"

"Because he might have been fun-loving and lacking a bit in the personal responsibility department, but Josh wasn't impulsive about important stuff. If he suspected his father was involved in something nefarious, he would have gotten his facts together before confronting him."

I pulled my legs up and wrapped my arms around my knees, resting my chin on them. "Okay, I'm with you so far. Where would he have started?"

"With Collen Landon, the victim's brother. He's been very vocal that he thinks Tomlinson killed his sister. What if Josh had contacted him and they'd agreed to meet?"

"Do you know where to find him?"

"Yep. He lives in Asheville. In fact, he owns one of the clubs Josh frequents."

"Okay, that seems important."

"Yeah. And I was thinking we should talk to him. Are you game?"

I didn't hesitate...though I definitely should have. "I am. When did you want to go?"

"No time like the present."

11

Illusions was located on Biltmore Avenue in downtown Asheville. As it was an extremely popular nightspot, the line to get in was all the way down the block and around the corner. Music pulsed out into the night through the open front doors. Light flashed colors over the excited faces of the clubbers in line. Conversations were lively and loud.

I eyed the long queue with trepidation, wondering if we'd make it inside before the sun started to rise in the sky.

Eddie didn't seem concerned. He clasped my hand in his big, warm grip and strode directly to the beefy bouncer standing in front of the gilded front doors. The man had an earpiece coiling from one ear and an intimidating glare fixed onto his wide face.

Eddie's smile smacked up against the bouncer's glare and pinged back off, unaccepted. But that didn't deter Deitz. He reached for the bouncer's big paw and gave it a couple of pumps while leaning close and whispering something into his ear.

A beat later, the man gave us a nod and motioned for the statuesque brunette at the door to let us through. She eyed Eddie as we moved past, her exotic almond eyes filled with invitation. Me, she sneered at like I was a particularly nasty type of bug. Eddie kept hold of my hand as we moved through the writhing crowd. Flailing hips, shoulders, and arms formed a vertical minefield that threatened bodily harm under the flashing lights. The music pulsed deep in my chest like a growl.

I stared around like a country girl who found herself in the city for the first time. It wasn't far from the truth. I didn't go out at night much. My previous excursions to late-night entertainment venues had mostly included dives with offbeat bands and one-dollar beer nights.

Cop bars.

At that moment, I realized just what a complete and utter dud I was. I was thirty-three years old, attractive, and had a certain kind of charm…if biting humor and self-deprecating wit could be called charming.

I needed to get out more.

Then I thought about what that would entail,

and weariness swept over me. There was a half-gallon of fudge ripple ice cream and a warm Pomeranian who thought he was a lion waiting for me at home. Who in their right mind wouldn't choose those things over three-inch heels that stabbed into their feet, music-induced deafness, and dance-generated eye-gouging hazards?

"Gah!" I mumbled to myself. "I'm old."

Eddie gave me a funny look and then shook his head. Leaning over the bar, he shouted something to the twelve-year-old behind it.

Which was further proof that I was old. Everybody in the bar looked like they'd just stumbled out of a preschool class and were soothing their teething gums on the ice in their plastic cups.

The pre-teen bartender pointed down the bar, where a handsome man stood staring morosely out over the roiling, rhythmic landscape, hands shoved into the pockets of his charcoal gray slacks.

Thank heavens. An adult. He had to be at least twenty-one.

Collen Landon fixed an unwelcoming stare on us as we fought our way down the bar. He skimmed a negligent look over Eddie and then let his gaze linger on me. Something about me must have caught his interest because he stopped looking morose for a moment and let humor tug his perfect lips upward at the corners.

I didn't fool myself that he was interested in me

in a physical way. He probably just enjoyed watching me stumble around in the unaccustomed heels. It *was* probably pretty entertaining since I resembled a very old toddler wearing her mother's shoes.

Eddie offered the other man his hand and leaned close to be heard above the music. "I'm a friend of Josh Mitner's. Do you think we could talk somewhere quieter?"

Landon's gaze never left mine. It narrowed a bit when Eddie made his offer, but he didn't show any other sign of having heard as he stared into my eyes.

Finally, he gave a small nod and turned away, moving through the crowd with liquid grace that put my clomping steps to complete shame.

He ascended a flight of stairs at the side of the big club and moved behind a wall of glass that cut the noise from below in a substantial way.

Only a few of the dozen or so tables on the second floor were occupied, and most of those people were too interested in each other to even notice our arrival.

Landon motioned toward a booth along the back wall and signaled to the waitress who was just settling a drink onto a nearby table. "What would you like?" he asked me in a deep, smoky voice.

As his voice soothed over me like warm maple butter, I suddenly wanted something that wasn't on the menu. My mind went blank. "Um…"

With both men's eyes on me, I swallowed self-consciously. "Just water, please."

Eddie requested something on draft, the name of which I didn't recognize.

We slid into the booth, Eddie on one side and me on the other. Landon slid in next to me.

His thigh briefly touched mine before I scooted away from it as discreetly as I could.

He looked at Eddie. "What's this about?"

"You heard about Josh's death?"

Landon frowned. "Josh who?"

The two men forged a battle of flashing gazes for a minute, during which time my water arrived. I gulped it like a woman who'd been lost in the desert for a month.

"I'm Josh Mitner's friend and a private investigator. I'm looking into his murder," Eddie finally said into the conversational void.

Landon blinked and looked up as the waitress put two icy mugs of beer in front of them. When she'd left, he took a moment to sip his beer. I got the impression he was playing for time. Finally, he settled the mug onto the table and leaned back. "Josh was killed?"

Eddie nodded.

Landon tapped a finger on the tabletop for a few beats and then expelled air in a rush. He ran his fingers through his thick mop of hair and closed his eyes for a beat. "I guess I should be worried."

"Tell me what Josh found out. I'm trying to help."

Landon shook his head. "I'll never know. He was meeting me here that morning while the club was empty. He said he'd found something out about Tomlinson that I needed to know."

"You have no idea what he discovered?"

"Only that he had a lead on the murder weapon."

"How was she killed?" I asked.

He glanced my way. "And you are?"

Heat filled my cheeks. "I'm sorry." I offered him my hand and introduced myself. "I'm working with Eddie on this." I didn't think it would help our case to tell him what my real job was. I could just hear our conversation...

You're a what?

I'm a fake mourner.

And you're investigating the death of the person you were fake-mourning? Why?

Um, I believe in going over and above in my work.

Uh-huh.

I was pretty sure he'd throw Eddie and me out of the club.

Landon drank more beer. "Her throat was slashed." He paled, his lips compressing as emotion rolled through him. "They haven't found the blade yet, and they won't tell me anything about it while the investigation is going on. But I know what

Tomlinson used to kill her. I gave it to her when she graduated from med school."

I felt my brows climb north on my face. "Your sister was a doctor?"

He gave me a proud smile. "On the way to becoming one of Asheville's finest surgeons. That's why I got her the scalpel."

"Scalpel?" Eddie asked.

Landon nodded. "An antique silver one with intricate markings on the handle. It was from the late 1800s and was worth some money. Not a lot, but more than just a regular scalpel. She loved that knife. Kept it locked up in a safe. She'd have brought it out to show him if he'd asked...otherwise...he probably wouldn't have even known she had it." Landon swallowed hard. "She trusted him." He shook his head. "I still can't believe he killed her."

"Why do you believe it was him?" Eddie asked.

"There's a ton of evidence against him," Landon responded. "But unfortunately, it's all circumstantial."

"Tell us," I urged.

He sighed. "Allie was dressed for a dinner out, her purse nearby and her keys on the floor close to the door as if the purse had gone flying and the keys had flown out of it. Her cell phone was underneath her body, the front crushed."

Eddie stopped him. "Crushed? From what?"

"It looks like a heel," Landon said. "The original

report had it down as damage that happened when she dropped and fell on it. But that's not possible. I saw the crime scene photos. That phone had been crunched under someone's heel, probably a wider heel like from a man's shoe."

"Okay, go on," Eddie said.

"No money was taken from her purse. Nothing that we can identify was taken from the home..."

"You mentioned a safe. Was it open?"

Landon shook his head. "No. And it seemed like everything was still inside."

"Everything except the scalpel," I reminded him.

"Right. That's still missing."

"Her throat was cut," Eddie prompted gently.

"It was. And there were defensive wounds on her palms." He swallowed hard. "She apparently put up quite a fight."

Something was bothering me about his account. "You said the police wouldn't tell you anything about the investigation. How do you know all this?"

He stared at his beer for a long moment. Finally, he said, "Josh sent me pictures. He got them from *Crime Clean's* database."

"Is that normal?" Eddie asked? "For the crime scene cleaning company to have crime scene photos?

Landon frowned. "Tell you the truth, I don't know. I just know he told me he could get in a lot of trouble if his dad knew he had them."

"Okay. What else?"

"Tomlinson was covered in blood...her blood... and his bloody fingerprints were everywhere."

"Was he there when she was attacked?"

"Of course, he says he wasn't."

"But he had her blood on him?" Eddie asked.

That seemed pretty straightforward to me. Tomlinson no doubt showed up for their date and tried to revive her. But I knew what Eddie was doing. He wanted all the facts in as straightforward a way as possible. Before we started pulling the pieces apart and trying to create a picture with them.

It's what any good cop would do.

"He claims he came to the house to pick Allie up for dinner and found the front door ajar. He came inside, calling her name, and saw the blood trail by the door..."

"Wait, where was your sister's body?"

"In the living room."

"Had she been dragged or moved?"

"Tomlinson claims not, but nobody can explain how that blood trail got on the tile of the entryway."

"Could it be the killer's blood?" I asked.

"No. It was Allie's."

I frowned. "Could it have dripped off Tomlinson? Maybe he went to the door to direct the police?"

"That's one of the options being considered, but from what Josh told me, the pattern isn't consistent with that."

"Maybe she fought with her attacker near the door. The blood could be from the defensive wounds."

Landon nodded. "That seems like the most likely scenario."

"Okay, so Tomlinson comes inside the apartment. He finds her body, bends over her, and checks her pulse..."

"He's not a doctor, so it seems unlikely he'd even know how to do that. TV and movie portrayals aside, it isn't the easiest thing to find a pulse," Landon said.

"CPR training?" I asked.

"Not that I know of. Tomlinson's a self-involved rich guy. He's not the type to take classes to learn how to save somebody else."

"You shouldn't assume that," Eddie said. "I'll check into it."

Landon frowned. "He's just so cool and arrogant. He barely even frowned when he was interviewed about her murder."

"You saw the interview?" I asked, surprised.

"Josh gave me that too."

I looked at Eddie. "There has to be a dirty cop."

He nodded.

"What do you mean?"

I sat forward, lowering my voice as the amorous couple from the nearest table stumbled past, wrapped around each other and heading for the stairs. "Let's assume *Crime Clean* is involved in hiding evidence for Tomlinson, a.k.a. the scalpel. The only reasonable way they could have gotten it was if the police didn't find it when processing the crime scene. It seems unlikely that would happen. But if you had a dirty cop...

Landon's eyes widened. "He could have held the evidence back until the scene was processed and then left it in some obscure place for the cleaning crew to find."

"Exactly."

I turned to find Eddie staring at me. "That's pretty smart, May."

I shrugged. "I'm surrounded by cops. They've spent lots of nights discussing murder and crime scenes over pizza and beer. I'm naturally nosy, so I pay attention."

Landon said with a smile. "Dinner and death. Yum."

I shared his smile. "Right? I can't get them to understand how disturbing that is."

"Well, it's led us to a pretty plausible reason for both the missing weapon and Alex Mitner's possible involvement in a cover-up. That would definitely explain why Josh might have been upset."

"And why he was helping me," Landon said.

"But there's one thing I don't understand," I told the two men. "Why wouldn't Tomlinson just hide the knife himself before calling the police?"

"Maybe he didn't have a chance," Landon told

her. "You aren't the only nosy one. Allie had a neighbor who paid attention to the comings and goings in the neighborhood. She saw Tomlinson stumble outside and throw up in the bushes about twenty minutes after he arrived. She noted the blood covering his fine suit and called the police. They arrived less than ten minutes later."

"Twenty minutes?" Eddie said. "That's a really long time to be inside the house if he wasn't killing her himself."

"Exactly," Landon responded. "He claims he was trying to revive her but, trust me, I saw those photos. There's no way if you walked in on someone who looked like that, you'd think she could be revived."

Eddie shook his head. "Grief does strange things to people."

Landon didn't respond.

I sat there thinking about the information Collen Landon had given us. Something about it was bothering me, but I couldn't quite figure out what it was.

Eddie stood up, offering the other man his hand. "Would you mind sending me that interview tape? I'd like to get a feel for our Mr. Tomlinson."

Landon stood too, forcing me to my feet. He nodded, taking the business card Eddie handed him. "Thanks for doing this," Landon said to both of us. "I've tried to dig into it but haven't gotten very far."

"Be careful," Eddie told the other man. "If Josh

was killed for poking around in this, you could be in danger too."

"Yeah, that's occurred to me. You be careful too," he addressed the last to me. I nodded.

"I'm really sorry for your loss," I told him. I seemed to be saying that a lot lately.

"Thanks."

Landon stayed behind as we descended the stairs to the club floor below. Behind the mask of the glass partition, I'd been lulled into thinking the noise and activity below had died down a bit. I couldn't have been more wrong. If anything, it had gotten worse. The floor was so packed there was barely room to move.

Which was one of the reasons I was surprised when we bumped up against a familiar face in the crowd.

12

"Hi, May."

   I gave James a tentative smile. "What are you doing here?"

   He laughed, shaking Eddie's hand. "I could ask you guys the same thing. I'm a regular. I've never seen you here before, Deitz."

   Eddie shrugged. He leaned close to shout in James' ear in an attempt to be heard over the noise. "May and I needed a little downtime." He grinned. "Did you just get here?"

   James skimmed me a look, his expression assessing. "About an hour ago. I've been holding court over there." He pointed toward a large round booth that was filled mostly with women. "You're looking particularly delectable tonight, Miss May."

   Heat filled my cheeks. I wasn't at all comfortable with the answering heat in his eyes. He was a very good-looking man, but something about him put me off my game. Maybe it was the fact that he'd had to save me from drowning not all that long ago. As a general rule, I was uncomfortable owing people favors. And saving my life was a pretty big one. "Thanks."

Eddie moved down to the step I was standing on, dropping a hand to the small of my back. It seemed a totally natural thing. Just a touch to remind me he was there, but I didn't miss the sharp exchange of looks between the two old friends.

"Would you like to sit with us?" James asked, looking at me.

I opened my mouth to refuse, but Eddie beat me to it. "No thanks. We were just heading out."

"Are you sure?" James shouted. "May looks like she wants to dance."

I realized I'd been swaying a bit to the music and forced my hips to stop moving. Before I knew what was happening, James had grabbed my hand and pulled me down the last two steps. He glanced at Eddie, laughing at my squeal of surprise. "I'll take good care of her, Deitz. No need to worry."

Somehow, I didn't think Eddie was worried about that. But judging by the way his jaw was clenched, he was definitely ticked.

At the edge of the dance floor, James swung me around and I landed in his arms, laughing breathlessly as we began to sway to music that was much too fast for the slow dance he'd engaged between us.

As if reading my mind, the music morphed into a nice, slow tune that lowered the volume in the club by several decibel levels.

I sighed with pleasure at not having my senses pummeled with sound.

It's possible James took my sigh as something else. He tucked me closer against his big body, his tall frame swaying under the sensual beat.

My feet had trouble finding the rhythm. Probably because my body was trying to put some distance between us.

After the third time I stumbled over his feet, he looked down at me, arching a brow.

I chuckled with embarrassment. "I'll just let you lead now," I told him.

His grin was wide. "I won't be threatened if you lead. But you'll need strong biceps to hold me in the dips."

Some of my stress fled as I laughed, shaking my head. "You can't take me anywhere."

His hand slipped warmly up my back, and he shook his head. "My bad; I kind of took you by surprise."

"You did. Why?"

He shrugged. "When I see something I like, I take it. I'm a take-charge kind of guy."

"You see, that's kind of a problem from my

perspective. I'm not a girl who likes someone taking charge of her."

"Noted. I'll be less take-chargy in the future." His handsome face turned serious. "You don't mind if there's a future, do you? I mean, maybe it's the whole saving you from drowning thing, or it could be seeing you in those very sexy fish flops the other night, but I find myself strangely drawn to you."

I laughed, thinking it was probably more from seeing me hanging half out of that undersized running suit. "I know when to break out the big guns to impress."

His wide grin was infectious. "How long have you known Deitz?"

I shrugged. "Not long. We met at Josh's viewing."

He looked surprised. "Really?" He glanced toward Eddie, who was leaning against the staircase with a fresh drink in his hand. He didn't look happy. "I have to give old Deitz some credit. I never pegged him as a 'pick up the pretty girl at the funeral' kind of guy."

I didn't let myself react to the pretty girl thing. We'd veered onto dangerous ground. "He didn't pick me up. He saved me."

"Saved you? From what? Terminable boredom? Oh wait, don't tell me you're allergic to lilies?"

I thought his joking about his old friend's funeral was inappropriate but wrote it off to him trying to be flirtatious. "He gave me a ride to the Mitner's after the viewing. My car was in the shop."

"Ah."

No way I was going to tell him about Mrs. Mitner's harsh words or my reluctance to climb into the limousine with the grieving couple. My clients' business was their own.

"Strange, huh?" When he gave me a confused look, I elaborated. "Josh dying that way. Getting hit in the wee hours of the morning by a trash truck." I watched him carefully. I wanted to know if he thought Josh's death was suspicious or if he hadn't given it any thought at all. Judging by his shrug and the way his gaze slipped up to the second level of the bar and stuck, I figured he was in group number two. Camp Clueless.

"We all have to die from something, right?" he finally said, dragging his gaze back down to mine.

I glanced up to where he'd been looking and spotted a gorgeous woman talking to Collen Landon at the top of the stairs.

You dog, I thought. He was scoping out other women while dancing with me. I did an internal head shake. Deitz had been right. It was unlikely James would kill his old friend over a woman. I doubted he'd ever invested more than pheromones and a bit of charm to conquer any woman.

But it wouldn't hurt to ask. "You and Josh were regulars here?"

"We are...were. Among other clubs."

"Did you usually come together?"

His eyes narrowed a little. "Occasionally. Why?"

"I just wondered if you shared the women."

When he blinked in surprise, I pointed to the oversized round booth. "That seems like too many dates for one man."

He laughed, shaking his head. "They're just friends. I fill in as a temporary boyfriend whenever one of them gets too much attention from someone they want to avoid."

"Ah. That's nice of you."

He shrugged again. "Nah. They do the same for me."

"Was Josh part of the fake date brigade too?"

"Yeah. Actually, he instigated it. Though he had a tendency to take it to the next level, if you know what I mean. Sometimes the pretending turned to something that wasn't so much pretend anymore. It got him in trouble once in a while."

"Trouble? How?"

James jerked his head toward the second floor. "You see that man up there?"

I glanced up as Collen Landon looked down, a frown furrowing his brow. "Yes."

"He owns this place. Sometimes his sister comes into the club. She's one fine-looking woman," James said. When I lifted my brows, he grew immediately defensive. "Not that I was looking to hook up or anything. She's definitely not my type."

"Oh? And what exactly is your type?" I wanted to kick myself as soon as the words came out of my mouth. They sounded way too much like flirting.

He seemed to take them that way too. Leaning closer, he placed his lips next to my ear and whispered huskily, "I prefer my women to wear googly-eyed fish shoes and form-fitting velour loungewear."

I flushed with embarrassment, shaking my head. "You were telling me about Mr. Landon's sister."

He looked at me kind of funny and then seemed to shake it off. "Well, Josh saw some guy manhandling her in here. A really aggressive guy who didn't seem to want to take no for an answer. She was trying not to make a scene, but the guy kept grabbing her arm and trying to drag her out of the club. Josh swept in and pretended to be her boyfriend, freshly returned from a bathroom run."

My eyes went wide as possibilities presented themselves in my mind. "What happened?"

"The guy punched Josh, laid him right out on the floor."

"Did Josh punch him back?"

"Nah. The bouncer showed up and threw him out."

"That's terrifying."

James shrugged. "Price of doing business, I

guess." He grinned. "Sometimes you have to lose a battle or two before you win the war."

"Did Josh win the war that night?"

"He did." James grinned. "The woman was very appreciative of his efforts. She and Josh spent the rest of the night dancing and drinking together."

I was dying to ask if they left together. If Josh had had a romantic relationship with Allie Landon, that might explain so much. I finally settled for a more generic question that I hoped would get me where I needed to be. "Did they date? Josh and Miss Landon?"

"Who knows?" James said, seeming to lose interest in our conversation. I caught him winking at a woman standing alone by the bar.

"What did the guy who was hassling her look like?"

His attention returned to me. "Why?"

I shrugged in what I hoped was a nonchalant way. "I'm just curious. Have you seen him around here again?"

"No. He didn't look like he belonged here. He was wearing a suit, and he was an older guy. Dark hair with gray on the sides. He looked rich. Funny way for a rich guy to act if you ask me."

The music stopped and James dropped my hand, giving me a smile. "Thanks for the dance. I guess I'd better let you go back to Deitz now before he decides to punch me in the nose."

"Thanks. It was fun." And I realized I wasn't completely lying. I had enjoyed the dance. But I'd enjoyed getting new information on the Landon case even more.

As Deitz moved toward me, his handsome face folded into a scowl, I wondered what that said about me. That I'd enjoyed the chance to solve a mystery more than I'd enjoyed dancing with a handsome, eligible man.

———

"L et's get out of here," I told Deitz. He didn't argue. In fact, I got the impression he was more than happy to comply.

We moved through the writhing mass of bodies as quickly as we could, Eddie's hand wrapped around mine to keep us from getting separated.

As we emerged into the relative silence of the night, I sucked in a grateful breath of air that didn't smell like a thousand clashing perfumes and enjoyed the quiet of the midnight streets.

The line of waiting clubbers had shortened considerably while we'd been inside and only a few cars moved along the streets, their headlights dancing off the buildings and skimming over us as they passed on by.

"I got new information from James," I told Eddie as we reached his truck.

"Really? Does he know something about Josh's death?"

"No." I slid inside and waited while Eddie walked around to the driver's side and climbed in. "But he knew something we didn't know about Josh and Allie Landon."

Eddie didn't make a move to start the truck. He turned in his seat to look at me. "What about them?"

"They might have been an item," I told him the story James had shared with me.

"Do you think James was telling the truth?" he asked when I'd finished.

I frowned. "That's a strange question. I don't know why he'd lie. It certainly wasn't going to get him lucky."

Eddie barked out a laugh. "Well, you have *him* figured out."

"This could change things, right? What if the guy bothering Allie was Tomlinson? What if he found out Josh and Allie had gone out? He could have killed them both in a fit of jealousy."

Eddie sat back and stared out the windshield of his truck, fingertips tapping the steering wheel as he thought. "That actually makes a lot more sense than what we were thinking." He finally nodded. "I'll call Landon in the morning and ask him if it was Tomlinson. I'm surprised he didn't mention it to us before."

"Yeah. Me too. But maybe he just forgot." It didn't

seem likely that he'd forget an encounter like the one James described since he believed Tomlinson killed his sister. But maybe he had some other reason for not telling us.

We drove back to my place in silence. Eddie pulled up to the curb in front of my building. My hand on the door handle, I turned to him. "You'll let me know?"

He shook his head and, for a minute, I thought he was saying he wouldn't let me know. But then he opened his door. "I'm not letting you walk upstairs by yourself. Not after everything that's happened."

I opened my mouth to argue, but he was already walking around the truck. And if I was honest with myself, I'd have to admit I was glad for the company.

I'd been too busy to think about it much, but when I did, the near-drowning and being chased through the cemetery had left me a little spooked.

Which probably accounted for the warm flush of pleasure that swept through me when Eddie's hand found the small of my back as he guided me safely to my door.

13

Shakes met me at the door, and I realized I'd forgotten to put him into the Pom Hilton before I left. I picked up the bouncing bundle of fur and let him cover my face with kisses. "You weren't a bad boy while I was gone, were you?"

Eddie reached out and scratched my furry little man behind one pert ear. "Bad? Like what, killing dust bunnies?"

I gave him slitty eyes. "I don't have dust bunnies."

"My point was, what possible trouble could he have gotten into while you were gone? He's four inches tall and probably weighs three pounds. I have dust bunnies in my apartment that could take him out without even breathing hard."

My lips twitched in a repressed grin. "Your dust bunnies breathe? Terrifying. You might need an exorcism or something."

"Har. You didn't answer my question."

I sighed. "Let me see. He could...poop or pee on the floor, chew the woodwork, eat the carpet, burrow into the space between the stove and the wall and get stuck, scratch at the door, eat the toilet brush..."

"Ew."

"Play with the television remote, de-stuff the couch cushions..."

Eddie's eyes went wide. "He's done that?"

"Turn his water bowl over and lay down in the water, bark at squirrels through the window, and annoy Doug..."

"Dude."

"Lick a giant wet spot on my pillow, scoot his butt over my comforter, 'hide' all his toys in the laundry basket..."

Eddie threw up his hands. "I give. Stop the torture. I'll tell you everything I know."

I grinned. "Too bad, I was just getting warmed up."

"Who knew something so small could get into so much trouble."

"I did."

Shakes barked happily, his fringe of a tail whipping the air behind him. "You need to go outside to potty? Okay, little man. Let me grab your leash." I settled him onto the floor, and he bounced happily toward the door, plopping onto his bottom to stare impatiently at me.

"He told you that, did he?"

"He did." I grabbed the leash off the hook on the wall behind the door and clipped it onto Shakes' Superman collar. I gave Eddie wide eyes. "Wait, are you telling me you don't speak Pomeranian?"

"It's not one of my current skills. But rest assured that I'm going to sign up for a class on it tomorrow."

I grinned. "If you can find that class, let me know. It would be worth the price of admission to watch you take it."

He snorted, pulling the door open. "Where do we walk the little guy?"

Shakes and I preceded him into the hallway. "Oh, you don't need to come. I'm sure you have better things to do."

He started to close the door and stopped. "You have your key?"

I pointed to the key dangling from the end of Shakes' leash.

"Genius," he told me.

"I try."

"As I believe I stated before, I'm not letting you walk around alone while we have a probable murderer out there."

I pretended annoyance but was secretly glad for the company. Shakes relished his potty walks. And I mean *relished*. He chose his targets more carefully than the CIA chooses its operatives. I'd never seen him select a spot to potty in shorter than twenty minutes. "This could take a while," I warned Eddie.

"I'm in it for the long haul."

"*Really* a while."

He pushed the exterior door open. "Should I grab my tent out of the truck?"

"It might be wise... wait, does it have inflatable beds? Shades might need to rest during his search for the perfect spot."

He laughed. We settled into a leisurely walk down the sidewalk, enjoying the sound of crickets that filled the air and the smell of onions cooking somewhere nearby. My stomach growled at the scent.

"Dude!" Eddie said, teasing me.

I flushed. "It must be ice cream o'clock."

He skimmed me a long look. "You don't strike me as a snacker."

"Shows what you know, Mr. Deitz. I live to snack. Snacking was my first and last name before I had to change it because it was too confusing for the post office."

His perfect lips curved upward. "Thank goodness you aren't one of those serial killers with three names then. The cops would be totally discombobulated."

"On the bright side, it would be easy to spell my name."

"Truth."

Shakes halted in a grassy spot beneath a large tree. Eddie and I stilled, watching expectantly.

But after a minute, he moved on. Apparently, the spot wasn't perfect enough to accept his biological donation.

Headlights skimmed over the tree behind us as Shakes bounced along the sidewalk, his tiny nose constantly shifting from side to side in search of a prime potty spot.

"I've always wanted a dog," Eddie told me.

I skimmed him a glance. "Really? Why don't you get one?"

He shrugged. "I'm gone a lot, stakeouts and stuff."

"Just take the dog with you."

He looked surprised. "I guess I could."

"Sure. Dogs love to go places with their humans. Plus, it would be good company. But you'd have to share your stake-out snacks."

Eddie shook his head. "And we're back to the snacks again."

Shakes plodded over to a bare spot of earth that held a single, tall blade of grass near its center. He sniffed loudly, his tail drooping slightly at whatever he smelled there.

We waited with bated breath, watching him peruse the spot. He circled the blade of grass three times and started to lift his leg.

Eddie and I did a fist bump.

Headlights lit up the night, catching the Pom in a wash of illumination that stopped his little leg in mid-lift.

"Dangit!" Eddie exclaimed in a truly heartfelt way.

Shakes whipped around and started barking at the car that eased slowly up to the curb behind us.

Eddie stiffened beside me. He took a half step to the side, moving between me and the vehicle as the lights snapped off and the car door opened.

I stepped around him and watched a man slide out of the driver's seat. He appeared to be about five-nine or ten, not a big guy, but he had broad shoulders and his arms were thicker than my legs. He looked strong.

There didn't appear to be anybody else inside the low-slung, two-door car. The sports car was silver with wide black racing stripes on the hood.

I jerked my chin toward the man as he strode toward us. "Nice car. 1973?"

He looked surprised. "Yeah. You know your Camaros."

"Some of them. My brother has one like it. Except his is bright orange."

The man and I shared a smile. "That's a little too conspicuous in my line of work."

"And what would that line of work be?" Eddie asked.

The man glanced at Shakes. "Hey, buddy."

Shakes growled low in his throat, his little body vibrating as he moved up next to me, his tail drooping. "He doesn't like strangers," I told the man. Though that was only a partial truth. He'd liked Eddie just fine when they'd met.

The man kept his gaze on Shakes and nodded. "Good dog. If they aren't willing to protect you, they're no better than house slippers."

I frowned at the house slipper reference. My dog might be small and furry, but he was a lion at heart. And he knew it too.

"You were about to tell us what line of work you're in..." Eddie reminded the guy.

"Ah. Sorry." He reached into the pocket of his jeans and Eddie flinched, his hands fisting. The guy noticed and stopped. "Just going for my badge."

"You're on the job?" I asked.

He nodded, holding the shield up to show us. "Detective Robard, APD."

"I assume you're here about the Tomlinson case?" Eddie said.

"You assume right."

"Why? And how did you find us?" I asked, picking Shakes up so he could quiver in my arms instead of on the ground.

"I understand you've been looking into the murder. I thought it made sense for us to share information."

A sudden sense of caution pattered across my

chest on tiny paws. Or maybe that was Shakes shoving his feet into me. "Sharing is nice. As long as it goes both ways. You have something that might help us figure out why Josh Mitner was killed?"

"I might. But I wanted to ask you what you know about Allie Landon's death first."

Eddie shook his head. "We don't know you. We have no reason to trust you, Detective Robard."

Robard gave us a tight smile. Lifting his hands to the sides, palms up, he said, "I'm an open book. Ask me anything."

Eddie jerked his head toward the car. "Okay, for starters, how did you find us here?"

"I saw you leave Ms. Ferth's apartment building and decided to follow at a discreet distance."

Well, that wasn't *too* creepy. "Why?" I asked.

"I just wanted to make sure I didn't lose you. I really wanted to have a chat."

"Why not approach us right away?" Eddie pressed.

"I didn't want to startle you. But it was taking so long I got impatient."

Eddie and I shared a smile. "You can't hurry a Pom," I told the cop.

"Apparently not." Robard's eyes narrowed as Shakes gave him another growl and curled his lip, showing tiny but sufficiently sharp teeth.

"Tell us about the Tomlinson case," Eddie

demanded. "Do you have enough to try him for the murder?"

Robard frowned. "It's all circumstantial. If we could find the weapon, we'd have him."

"Where do you think it is?" I asked.

"Heck if I know. I was hoping you or the brother could shed some light on that."

"You spoke to Collen Landon?" Eddie asked. "Is he the one who told you about us?"

"Not yet, no. He's next on my list. But he's been very open about his belief that his sister was killed with an antique scalpel he bought her."

"Yeah, he told us the same thing," I offered. "It still hasn't been found?"

"Unfortunately, no." His gaze narrowed on Eddie. "What can you tell me about Mitner's company, *Crime Clean*?"

It was all I could do not to glance at Eddie. It seemed the Asheville PD had made the same connection we had.

"Not much. Josh has told me stories."

"What kind of stories?"

"Nothing that would help you with the Tomlinson case. Just interesting scenes they've worked."

Robard nodded. He looked at the ground for a moment, his jaw flexing as if he were literally chewing something over. Finally, he looked up. "Has he mentioned a guy named Sugar Morellis?"

Eddie frowned. "The cartel leader? What are you...?" Eddie's eyes went wide. "You think Alex Mitner has a deal with the cartel to scrub evidence?"

Robard just stared at him.

I opened my mouth to tell him my 'dirty cop' theory. Eddie's arm lifted slightly, bumping me. I realized it hadn't been an accident and slammed my mouth closed.

"How well do you know Mitner?"

"Not that well. He asked me to do a job for him recently."

Robard didn't look surprised. I realized that was the real reason he'd come looking for us. He thought Eddie might be working for Alex Mitner.

"What kind of job?"

Eddie stared at the cop for a long moment and then relaxed, shoving his hands in his jeans pockets. He actually smiled. "I think you already know the answer to that."

Robard expelled air. "You spent some time checking up on Mr. Tomlinson. Why would Mitner want you to check up on him?"

"Honestly? I have no idea."

I chewed on the inside of my lip, hoping my expression was neutral. Robard turned to me, his brown gaze narrowing. Clearly, he knew who the weak link was in the partnership. It took everything I had, but I managed not to say anything.

"What did you find out?" I thought Robard was

talking to Eddie, though his gaze stayed glued to my face.

My palms were starting to sweat. Shakes was growling again, his tiny chest vibrating against my hand.

He really didn't like Robard.

"Are you aware that *Crime Clean* was the company that cleaned up after Allie Landon was killed?"

"That seems like a huge coincidence," Eddie said in a neutral tone of voice.

"It does, doesn't it?" Robard responded. "What kinds of things did Mr. Mitner ask you to find out about Tomlinson?"

Eddie shrugged. I marveled at his seeming indifference. Shakes and I were a jumble of nerves, and we weren't even being grilled. "The usual stuff. Financials, activities, police record, known associates."

"I find it interesting that you didn't think to ask him why he wanted you to investigate a man he was doing business with."

If Eddie caught Robard's insinuation, he didn't react.

"I wasn't aware he was currently doing any business with Mr. Tomlinson. I assumed he was looking at him for a future venture of some kind. Mr. Mitner has several partners. You don't sustain a successful business in multiple states across the country without business partners."

"Why would an educational book publisher want to partner with a crime scene cleaning company?"

"Diversification?" Eddie offered in the form of a question. Then he smiled, and Robard's jaw tightened.

"I know where you've been sticking your nose, Deitz. I know you sniffed around some pretty low places filled with questionable people."

"Then I guess you don't need me, do you? You seem to already know it all."

Shakes barked, his tail whipping happily as if to say, *touché*!

Robard's lip curled. "I think I'll just stop by the local precinct and talk to the supervising Lieutenant of the Hazardous Devices Team. The cop glanced my way. "I believe you know him?"

I'm pretty sure my neutral expression wavered a bit on that one. But I was proud of my voice when I responded. It didn't quiver at all. "Say hey for me. And tell him I might be late for dinner tomorrow night. I'm going to have another busy day."

I was pretty sure Robard's teeth were grinding together when he turned away. Eddie and I watched him drive his sexy Camaro past and away before Eddie spoke. "Well, that was interesting."

"What is a Detective from the mean streets of

Asheville doing here in the 'burbs, harassing private citizens?" I asked rhetorically.

"I don't know, but I'm going to find out. I made some connections when I was there. I need to know what Robard's looking for and if we can trust him.

"Or if we just met our dirty cop," I finished for him.

14

The next morning I had to go to Exit Stage Left for a Mitner job debrief with Ruthie. It wasn't standard practice on an assignment, but since so much had happened, I thought it would be a good idea to fill my boss in on my part in all of it.

Kind of a cover-my-butt thing.

I kissed Shakes on the tip of his tiny, wet nose and placed him inside the Pom Hilton, giving him a dog cookie before closing the door. "Be good, handsome."

He barely spared me a glance as I left, his full attention on the cookie he'd already crushed into crumbs.

I climbed into Betty, patting her fondly on a well-worn dash before starting her up. Her oft-rebuilt engine rumbled throatily, making me smile. My girl was a bit dinged and age-spotted with rust, but she had a heart of gold and the engine of a studly young race car.

I selected a song from the playlist on my phone and cranked the volume up as I hit the highway into town. The sun had barely been up an hour, and already the beautiful North Carolina morning was succumbing to its steamy influence. I could have put the air conditioning on, but I preferred to enjoy the warm sweetness of the flower-drenched air on my drive.

Exit Stage Left was located in a shopping mall with the Smoky Mountains rising majestically in the background. The agency was nestled between a boutique and a florist, and there was also a gourmet bakery and a large office store down the way.

I parked and locked Betty, heading toward the gray brick building that housed Exit Stage Left. My nostrils flared under the decadent scents of the gourmet bakery. I forced myself to keep walking, determined not to succumb to the siren song of buttery pastries and rich, dark coffee.

At least until after my business was done.

The bell on the door jingled softly as I opened it. Ruthie looked up as I entered. She sat behind her white receptionist's desk, peering down at a client folder, the contents of which were spread across the messy desk.

Ruthie peered at me over sixties-style glasses, which had been missing a few rhinestones since the first day I met her. I was pretty sure she'd had been wearing those glasses since the sixties, and I was also betting they'd still be on her face a dozen years from now.

"Hey, Ruthie."

Her faded blonde hair had been stretched into its usual topknot, the strands pulled so tight I doubted she'd ever have need of a facelift. She was dressed in a cardigan that was a slightly yellowed white, and it hung a bit crookedly over a flowered cotton dress that looked like it might have gone to parties with Ruthie's glasses in the sixties. "May," she growled out in her whiskey and tobacco voice. "I'm a little worried you wanted to talk. Should I be expecting a call from an irate or otherwise unhappy client?"

I shook my head and sat down in the hard chair across from Ruthie. "I just wanted to let you know that I managed to finish out all of my tasks for the assignment, despite some real challenges."

She shoved the glasses up her nose and sniffed. "That's good because I just sent Alex Mitner a bill for the full spectrum of services."

I nodded. "He'll pay it. I don't expect any issue there."

She cocked her head, and I wondered if it hurt to

have her cheeks yanked backward into her hairline by the sturdy twist of hair on the top of her head.

Then I figured all the nerves in her face had probably succumbed to stress injuries years ago.

"But there *was* an issue, wasn't there?"

I nodded. "Several, actually. I told you about being accused of killing Josh myself and subsequently spraying my accuser with mace..."

Ruthie nodded. "Unfortunately, yes."

"I'm really sorry about that."

She nodded but surprisingly didn't look all that concerned. After an unknown number of years in the professional mourning business, she'd probably heard it all. Her next words confirmed it. "It's happened before."

"Good."

"You convinced him otherwise, though, right?"

"Um..."

Ruthie pursed her lips. She would have been the one to do the research and put together the information in the dossier she gave me. "Everything I learned about Josh Mitner said he was a player. It wouldn't have been unusual for him to date a woman and not tell anybody."

I shrugged. "I must have a shifty look about me."

I didn't get the smile from Ruthie I'd hoped for. But that wasn't unusual. Ruthie rarely smiled about anything except the receipt of money. The bigger the payout, the wider her smile.

"But at least he knows better now, right? You set him straight?"

I hesitated a bit too long.

"MayBell?" The warning in her tone was clear.

I flinched. "I did. Multiple times. But he didn't buy it. He's a naturally suspicious person."

She sighed. "Is this going to be a problem?"

"No. He understands I was just doing a job. He won't say anything to anybody."

She lifted a graying blonde eyebrow. "How can you be so sure?"

Again, I hesitated a beat too long.

She sighed. Long and hard. "What am I going to do with you, May?"

I tried a smile. It was a weak attempt. "Trust me?"

"You can't be having relationships with mourners, May. You know this. It's rule number one."

"Number three, actually." Ruthie had a lot of rules. She sometimes got them mixed up.

When she glared across the desk at me, I flinched. "Sorry. It's not like that. We're not involved. He just asked me to help him prove Josh was murdered."

Ruthie's face turned chalky. She wobbled a bit as if she was going to pass out. I wasn't fooled. Her professional mourners weren't the only ones who tended to embrace drama. "You're working with him? As a PI?"

I decided a partial truth was better than an

outright lie or, gasp, the ugly reality. "I told him I wouldn't help."

She sat back hard in her chair. "I'm lost in the maze that is your mind."

I chewed the inside of my lip. I couldn't exactly tell her that I was helping him because I found myself in the crosshairs of a killer. "I'm not working as a PI. I'm just a sounding board for him. He knows I have a police background."

She lifted both brows on that one. "Background? Either you neglected to mention that on your resume, or I'm losing my mind. I don't remember the bullet point in the *Experience* section where it stated you'd been a cop."

"Obviously, I haven't. But I'm surrounded by them. I've kind of picked up some stuff over the years. You know," I finished weakly. Things were not going well. At that point, I figured the best thing I could do was get out while the getting was good. I stood up so fast my chair wobbled. "Anyway, I wanted to let you know the assignment was complete, and Alex Mitner seems pleased with the results." Of course, I didn't tell her that Mrs. Mitner was far less than pleased. No sense digging the hole any deeper.

Said the girl using a rhetorical backhoe to rip a car-sized hole for herself to fall into.

"May...?"

I waved jauntily. "I need to go prep for my next assignment. Talk to you later."

"You'd better not be investigating a murder!" Ruthie yelled after me as I hightailed it out of the office.

I hit the sidewalk and stopped, one hand on my twirling stomach and the other on the warm gray brick beside the door. The way my heart was pounding, I was pretty sure investigating a murder wasn't going to be a problem.

I was going to drop dead of a heart attack well before I investigated anything.

My phone rang as I was sliding back into Betty. I looked at the ID and saw it was the Lieutenant. I quickly hit *Ignore*. The last thing I needed was to have a repeat of the conversation I'd barely survived with Ruthie. And if Robard had spoken to him as he'd threatened, my standing was going to be even weaker with my dad. He'd make my life miserable if he found out what I was doing with Deitz.

As if thinking his name had conjured him up, my cell rang again and Deitz's name popped up. I answered quickly. "Hey."

"Hey yourself. Are you okay?"

"Fine. Why?"

"I've been a little uneasy about Robard showing up. I contacted my sources in APD, and the news isn't good."

I laid my head on the steering wheel. "Really? What's wrong?"

"He's known as a bit of a rebel. Likes to color outside the lines. And once he gets his teeth into something, he never lets go until he's figured it out."

"Awesome."

"Yeah. I was thinking we maybe should try another tack."

"I'm listening."

"I might have a job for you. But I'm warning you. You're probably not going to like it."

"You want me to what?" I shrieked in a decidedly unladylike manner.

"You're an actress. You can pull this off," Eddie told me.

"It's one thing to act a part and quite another to pluck one off the carpet and put it into a bucket."

"You won't be plucking any parts off the carpet, May. By the time you arrive on the scene, the police will have already removed all the...erm...parts."

"Tell that to Allie Landon and her brother."

"Come on, work with me here."

I sighed. "Okay, but this is a one-time deal. *One* crime scene. *If* it's necessary. And hopefully, it won't be a grisly one."

He arched a brow, his lips compressed. "What do you consider grisly?"

"Guts, excessive blood, any type of bodily fluids, and definitely no severed fingers or random brain parts."

"Okay," his very sexy mouth finally gave up the fight to stay neutral. "...you're thinking something along the lines of death by paper cut?"

I fought to hold my outrage, but it was getting harder by the minute. I was even amusing myself. "As long as the cut is really small and there's minimal blood."

He laughed, shaking his head. "Here." He handed me a dossier that looked suspiciously like the ones I got from Ruthie. "I've created everything you need...resume, customer testimonials, website..."

"Wait, you created a website?" I was impressed despite myself.

"Just a landing page, really. But it will do the trick. The phone number on the site is for this phone..." He handed me a burner phone. "I've already gotten you an interview. It's in an hour..."

"An hour!" I squeaked. "I need time to get into character."

"Go scrub a toilet or something. Really, all you need is to have experience cleaning. They won't expect you to know the finer points of crime scene cleaning. They have special cleaners and methods they'll teach you."

"Scrub a toilet?" I asked, appalled. "I'm not sure I'm up for this assignment."

"Don't tell me you've never scrubbed a toilet."

I winced. "My own, yes. But somebody else's…" I chewed my lip. "I have a slight case of porcelain phobia."

Eddie barked out a laugh. "Well then, unless your victim was killed while reading the newspaper on the toilet, you should be fine."

"I can't believe I let you talk me into this." I had a sudden thought. "What about Mr. Mitner? If he sees me, I'll be toast."

"He won't see you. I happen to know he golfs every Monday morning." Eddie eyed my worried face. "Don't look so grim. You'll probably never even work a scene. I just want you to see if you can find anything out from the inside."

"What about you? What are you going to be doing?"

"I'll keep watch to make sure Mitner doesn't return too soon. If he does, I'll head him off and keep him busy. If I send you a text that says *Flush*, you need to skedaddle out of there, preferably through a back exit."

"Flush?" I asked, hands on hips.

He grinned. "Just trying to speak your language."

Shaking my head, I shooed him out the door, so I

could read quickly through the dossier before getting dressed and heading out to the local office of *Crime Clean*.

Which presented me with the next problem. How did one dress to scrape blood and guts off the carpet?

15

An hour later, I entered the offices of *Crime Clean* and stood there, looking around. The office wasn't exactly what I'd expected, but it was close. A single palm tree arched from a large pot in the corner, the room's only spot of color. The furnishings were of good quality but sparse. Along one wall was a gray-washed wood desk with a receptionist behind it. The opposite wall held four black leather chairs for guests. The walls and carpet were white, and the only paintings were enlarged photos of the *Crime Clean* team and some of the Asheville Police Department personnel they worked with. It occurred to me that Detective Robard might be in one of the pictures.

"Can I help you?"

My gaze jerked to the young woman sitting behind the desk. She wore white overalls with a hot pink tee shirt. Her hair was styled in shoulder-length black braids with beads interwoven through the braiding. She had a small gold loop through one nostril, and a tiny tattoo of a rose on her throat, just above the vee neckline of her tee. Unlike her surroundings, she was nothing like I'd expected. "Hi. Um, I'm here to talk to Brad."

Two lines appeared between the receptionist's midnight brows. She looked at her computer screen. "Did you have an appointment?"

"Yes. Mabel Froth," I winced internally at the name. Who called themselves *Froth* if they had a choice? I sounded like a bad mug of beer or the bottom half of a ballet tutu.

Eddie told me he'd chosen the name to be as close to my real name as possible so I wouldn't get confused.

"Oh, there it is. Brad's running a little late this morning. You can wait over there. Would you like something to drink?"

I didn't recoil, but I wanted to. The last thing on my mind in that place was eating or drinking anything. Not when there might be blood-spattered porcelain in my near future.

The thought made my stomach twist with dread.

"No thanks. I'm good."

While I waited for the elusive Brad, I scanned the pictures on the wall. Though I had no idea what I was looking for, I told myself I'd know it when I saw it. Sure enough, when I got to the third picture, I spotted Detective Robard standing next to Alex Mitner, both men grinning widely.

"Miss Froth?"

It took me a beat to realize someone was talking to me. Taking a quick, deep breath, I closed my eyes and let the persona I'd cultivated slide into place.

I turned with a smile.

The man who approached me wasn't very big. He was probably only about five feet seven or eight inches tall and had dull brown hair, worn just past his ears and ruler-straight. It skimmed his wide brow in an unbroken fringe and split over largish ears that poked out from his head, making the fine strands of hair stick out too.

His angular face was covered in freckles and his mouth was small, the bottom lip plumper than the top. With his slightly bulgy brown eyes, he looked like a puffer fish with bad hair.

"I'm Brad."

I nodded, taking his offered hand. "May...bel Fr..."

He watched me like someone might watch a spider as it spins its web. Fascinated as I seemingly struggled just to give my name.

"...erm...Froth. It's nice to meet you."

Brad's lips turned up the minimum amount needed to count as a smile. "Come on back to my office and let's talk."

I followed Brad through a door and into a hallway with linoleum floors and plain white walls. Though spectacularly unadorned, the space was pristine and the air smelled fresh, with a citrusy scent.

Brad's office was hardly bigger than a good-sized supply closet. Most of the space was taken up by a metal desk, whose surface held several tidy stacks of folders with names and case numbers scrawled across the fronts. The floor and just about every other available surface was covered in cleaning equipment and supplies. There was a single black leather chair like the ones in the waiting room in the corner. Brad quickly removed a bucket filled with cleaning supplies from the chair and swiped a hand over the seat, glancing apologetically in my direction. "Sorry for the mess. It's been extremely busy this week. I haven't had time to straighten up."

"Lots of crime in Asheville?" I asked with a grin.

To my surprise, he nodded. "Mostly domestic stuff, but yeah."

He indicated the chair. "Sit. Can I get you something? A bottle of water or some coffee?"

"No thanks."

He dropped into his desk chair and opened the file in front of him. I assumed the folder held my resume and associated documents that Eddie had put together. "You've had your own cleaning business for five years?" he asked without looking up.

"Yes."

"With three employees?"

"That's right."

He looked up from my stats. "Why have you decided to join *Crime Clean*?"

Warming up to my persona, I gave him a sad smile. "I feel like I need to do something important, you know? I have friends who are police officers, and the work they do is so vital. I respect them for it. Unfortunately, to be honest, I'm kind of a scared little bunny when it comes to danger. But cleaning... that I can do. In fact, I'm pretty darn good at it, if I must say so myself."

He held up a sheet of paper. It looked like an email he'd printed. "Fortunately, you don't have to say so yourself. I have a list of happy customers here."

"My references?" I asked innocently.

"Yes. We like to get a feel for the type of people we're hiring. The culture can be...difficult. But we're a family. We help each other succeed and look out for one another. Only a certain type of person will fit into this climate."

I allowed myself to chew on my lip a little as if I was worried they wouldn't select me. Leaning closer, I placed a hand on top of the desk. "I'd heard that. It's why I really want to work here. This sounds like exactly my kind of place."

Brad nodded, narrowing his brown gaze. He sat

back in his chair and looked me in the eye. "You said you have friends on the force?"

"Yes..." The next part was a bit tricky. Deitz and I had discussed it at length and decided it was worth the risk. "Do you know Detective Robard?"

Brad's gaze widened slightly. His hand fell on my folder, fingers flicking the corners of my resume.

I held my breath, uncertain how to read his actions. Finally, he inclined his head and smiled. "I do know him. He happens to be a good friend of our owner's. The detective is our go-to when we need something from the APD."

He looked down at my resume. I held my breath. Our ploy would only work if they didn't contact Robard directly to ask him about me. I had no doubt they'd do it eventually, but I figured I'd be long gone by then. Because of the risk, Deitz had done some preliminary checking. We'd discovered that Robard was generally off work on Mondays. Our hope was that he'd be unreachable until the following day.

Still, a little distraction wouldn't hurt. I leaned close, lowering my voice as if providing a tidbit of something confidential. "I ran into the Detective the other evening. I was walking my dog, and he stopped to say hi. He mentioned he's working the Tomlinson case. Did *Crime Clean* work that scene?"

If I'd been worried about generating suspicion on Brad's part by asking directly about a case, I needn't have been. He plumped up like a banty rooster. Clearly, he liked talking about his work. "We did. Between you and me, that one was a mess. I'm not even surprised the police couldn't find the weapon. By the time they got there, Mr. Tomlinson had trod all over the evidence, touched just about everything in the place, moved the body, and puked in the bushes to top it off." He shook his head. "It was Detective Robard's worst nightmare."

"I can imagine. That poor young woman. I heard her brother's raising quite a stink."

Brad's lips curled. "We don't get involved in that end of things, of course, but in this case, I can't help feeling a bit protective. The brother all but accused the *Crime Clean* techs of removing the murder weapon from the scene."

I let my eyes go wide. "Seriously? That's so wrong."

Brad nodded enthusiastically. "I know, right? But there's nothing they can prove. The APD signed off on the scene before we went in. Ultimate responsibility falls on them. But if they did miss something, which happens occasionally. I mean, we're all human, right?"

"Right," I agreed.

"If they did miss something, we would have found it and turned it into the officer in charge."

"Robard?" I asked innocently.

"Yep. I worked that scene myself, and I can tell you without a smidgen of doubt that there was nothing there—no weapon of any kind. We would have found it.

"But you didn't go over the entire house, right? Just the scene of the death?"

"That's true. Our work was restricted to the lower level. I guess it's possible the weapon could have been hidden upstairs. But the police went over the entire house with a fine-tooth comb." He shook his head. "Detective Robard is very thorough."

"I respect that about him. And he spoke so highly to me about this company. I'd be proud to work here."

Brad beamed.

I gave him a conspiratorial look. "I've actually been following the case in the news. It's fascinating. I guess any time you brush up against the wealthy and famous, it's just a little more interesting."

He shrugged as if he was unaffected, but his eyes sparkled.

I glanced around and then lowered my voice further. "Have you met him? Do you think he killed her?"

Brad frowned. For a beat, I thought I'd gone too far. But then he leaned closer, his eyes shining. "I believe Tomlinson probably did kill her. But the police will never prove it. He's too smart for that."

"Seriously? That's horrible. What do you think happened to the weapon?"

Brad shrugged, seeming to lose interest. But I

saw the sudden stiffness in his weak jaw that told me he was feeling defensive. "He hid it somewhere. He had a few minutes after he called the police. Even more time *before* he called them."

I nodded. "I heard he didn't call them for over twenty minutes after he found her. That's plenty of time to hide the weapon."

He nodded. "That's what we thought too. Mr. Mitner said the neighbor called the police before he did."

"What in the world was he doing in the house all that time?"

"Stomping all over the evidence for one," Brad said, shaking his head.

"Do you know what's really interesting?" I asked him.

He cocked his head to indicate attentiveness, so I went on. "Despite the fact that the police only have him on circumstantial evidence that probably won't hold up in court, I haven't heard anybody speculating about other possible perpetrators. You'd expect more than one suspect on a case this big. Like an ex-boyfriend or a home robbery gone wrong. Something..."

He nodded thoughtfully. "You're right. I hadn't thought about that. Mr. Mitner seems convinced that Mr. Tomlinson's innocent, but even *he* hasn't mentioned any other suspects."

"Is Mr. Mitner the owner of *Crime Clean*?" I asked just so I didn't appear to know too much.

"Yes. He's quite the crime aficionado. He follows all the cases we get involved in very closely. And he's really good at figuring out the guilty party. We like to tease him that he should have become a cop."

"I suppose most people in this profession are interested in crime. It would be hard not to be, right?"

"Yep. That's true." Seeming to lose interest in our conversation, Brad stood up. "Okay, there's some preliminary stuff we need to get done, of course. You'll need to take a drug test, and we'll run a background check on you. But I'm sure all that will come back fine." He handed me a sheet of paper. "In the meantime, we can get started on your training. Why don't you fill out that form authorizing us to begin? I'll go check the training schedule? I think there's an entrails and brain matter collection lecture this afternoon. You could probably start there."

I gagged a little, keeping my head down so he wouldn't see.

He left me to my form. Unfortunately, he'd just closed the door behind him when my cell dinged with a text message. I looked down at it and saw a single word that sent chills slicing through me.

Flush!!!

Grabbing my purse, I cast a quick look over the folders on the desk and sent a longing glance toward the file cabinet behind Brad's desk. I'd love to get hold of the folder for the Tomlinson case.

Voices approached the office door, and I recognized one of them. I swear I could feel all the blood fleeing my face. I stood there for a beat, unsure what to do, and then gave in to the strongest impulse. Hurrying across the room, I opened the bottom drawer of the cabinet, my fingers doing a quick walk through the files in the "T" section.

There was no folder marked with the name Tomlinson. Either it was on Brad's desk, or it had already been removed. I closed the drawer again as quietly as I could and stepped to the desk, shifting the folders of the first pile enough to read all the names.

No Tomlinson.

Brad's voice sounded outside the door. My pulse kicked up into stroke range.

I straightened the first pile and did an even quicker look through pile number two.

The doorknob started to turn and then stopped as a woman's voice interrupted Brad's conversation with another man.

Watching the knob, I quickly sifted through the third pile.

I barely made it back to my seat and started scribbling my name on the form before the door opened and Brad the pufferfish doppelganger came inside, holding a brochure in his hand. "You're in luck. They have room in this afternoon's lecture."

I looked up from my form and gave him what I hoped was a sincere smile. It wasn't easy with my lips contracting in horror. "That's great."

He nodded toward the form I was not filling out. "As soon as you finish that, I'll take you around and introduce you to everybody. Mr. Mitner just got in. It's your lucky day. He's usually not here this early on Mondays."

"Yay, me," I said with as much enthusiasm as I could muster.

He nodded, oblivious. Moving around behind his desk, Brad frowned down at the piles of folders. Panic flashed through me. It didn't help when my cell dinged with another text.

I glanced down at my lap and saw the series of question marks from Deitz. If I didn't get out of there *tout de suite*, he was going to be coming in.

"I..." My mind swirled with a reason to leave the office, finally settling on the simplest excuse. "Could you tell me where the ladies' room is? I'm afraid I had one too many cups of coffee this morning." I grimace-smiled at him, and he chuckled.

"Down the hall to the left."

"Thanks." Scurrying toward the hallway as quickly as I could, I plunged through the door just as Brad reached out and shoved a corner of one of the piles, his gaze lifting speculatively to me as I pulled the door quickly closed.

I headed toward the exit sign at the end of the hall, hoping it would lead me to a back door out of the office.

Spotting the ladies' room as I heard voices coming from the other direction, I hesitated while considering ducking inside for a moment.

I shouldn't have hesitated.

"May?"

I jerked to a stop, my heart trying to leap out of my throat, and closed my eyes. Then I did the only thing I could.

Fixing a surprised look on my face, I turned around to face the man walking toward me down the hall.

16

J ames' gaze was narrowed, his smile tentative. "We meet again. I'm going to start thinking you're following me."

My answering laugh was weak.

What are you doing here?" he asked.

I sifted through my memories, trying to recall if I'd ever told James what I did for a living. I didn't think it had ever come up. "I...um...I'm applying for a job."

His expression closed a tiny bit more. "Really? Does Alex know?"

I frowned. "Why? Do you think he'd oppose the idea?"

James' suspicious expression smoothed away. He seemed to belatedly realize how his question had sounded. "Not at all. I really don't know what he'd think. I'm guessing because of your relationship with Josh, he'd think it was a good idea."

I nodded. "Josh is the reason I decided to apply. He used to talk about *Crime Clean* with such enthusiasm."

James' gaze narrowed again, and I realized my mistake. Eddie had told me that Josh was ambivalent about the company. If James was as close to the family as he appeared, he'd probably know that.

"I know, he wasn't always thrilled about following in his dad's footsteps..." I chuckled, and James lifted his brows in seeming agreement. "But he respected the work they did here. To tell you the truth, I'd feel like I was doing something important at *Crime Clean*."

"I get that," James admitted. His broad shoulders seemed to relax a fraction.

"What are you doing here?" I asked, skimming a look toward Brad's door. I was silently willing him not to come looking for me. Hopefully, his sensibilities would be too great to interrogate me about what I'd been doing in the bathroom for so long.

"I work for Alex."

"Oh? I didn't know that." I took a risk by adding, "Josh didn't mention it."

"It hasn't been for long. Just a couple of weeks."

Just before Josh was killed. I nodded. "Are you a crime cleaner?" I grinned.

"No thanks," he laughed huskily. "My business is

Security." He reached into the pocket of his polo-style shirt, extracting a business card and handing it to me. "If you ever need protection."

"Thanks."

"I'm sure you won't. But you never know." He lifted a dark brow. "Of course, you could always just use the number on the card to call me. You know, for other reasons."

With a shock, I realized he was flirting again. I'd written it off the last time to James trying to get under Eddie's skin. "Oh. Yeah. I might do that."

Dangit! I should never have said that. It would do no good to lead him on.

"Good." He glanced down the hall. "I should get back. Alex and I have to talk about adding some additional security to the building." He reached out and grasped my hand, squeezing it. "It was really nice seeing you again. Let's stay in touch."

I nodded and watched him walk back the way he'd come. My mind shuffled through the reasons Alex Mitner might employ a security company. They were obvious and not necessarily connected to Josh's murder. But the timing was really suspect. And it made me wonder what Alex was concerned enough about to hire James. It seemed the threat he'd had Eddie investigating hadn't abated with Josh's death. Shaking myself out of my thoughts, I spun on my heel as my cell dinged again, and I glanced down. *Eddie.*

I'm coming in!

I quickly typed a response. *No. I'm coming out now.*

———

Deitz glared at me as I pulled open the truck door and climbed inside. "It's about time! I was having kittens and a cow out here."

I shook my head. "Don't even try to compare your stress level to mine." I slammed the door. "Drive. I want to put some distance between myself and this place."

"That bad, huh?"

I held up a finger and thumb with very little space between them. "I came this close to having to learn how to collect entrails and brain matter."

"Bleurgh!"

"Exactly. And as you know, Alex Mitner is inside. But you'll never guess who else..."

A knock sounded on my window. Eddie and I jerked around.

James was staring through the glass at us. He didn't look amused.

I sighed. "Apparently, now you don't have to guess."

Eddie hit the window button and it slid down. "Hey man, what a surprise."

James glared at me, slowly skimming the glower to Deitz. "Unlock the doors."

Eddie frowned. "Why...?"

"Do it!" James demanded.

I opened my mouth to argue, but his scowl burned me like the sun's unfiltered rays. I snapped my lips shut.

There was a soft click, and the back door opened. James slid inside. "Drive."

Eddie did as he was told, his expression carefully neutral. "Where to, Miss Daisy?"

"There's a diner about a mile up on the right."

Silence throbbed through the truck as we drove the short distance. I had to clamp down on myself several times as excuses popped up and begged to be let out to fill the silence. But I knew I'd only bury us deeper if I tried to explain. I decided to wait until Eddie said something and take my cue from him.

If there was anything I was good at, it was taking cues.

Nobody spoke until we were seated in a chrome and red vinyl booth at a really cute retro-style diner. Eddie and I sat on one side and faced our stone-faced accuser.

James and Eddie ordered coffee. I ordered a diet soda. I was dying for a piece of the banana cream pie showcased in the refrigerated case near the door, but it just didn't seem like a pie kind of meeting.

Too bad. That pie looked outstanding.

"Tell me what you two are up to."

Eddie didn't appear cowed by James' strongman tactics, but he also didn't try to lie his way through it. Which, I'll admit, surprised me a little.

"We think Josh was murdered."

James didn't look surprised. "And?"

Eddie glanced at me. I felt my eyes go googly. "You knew," I accused James.

"Why do you think Mr. M's updating the security at work and home?"

At that point, I was pretty sure my eyes resembled the eyeballs on my fish flops. "Is Mrs. Mitner in danger?"

"Until we figure out who's threatening them, everybody's in danger." He held my gaze. "Including you two, apparently."

I couldn't shake the feeling he knew about the attempts on our lives. Then I realized he most certainly knew about the incident at the Mitner's. "You knew the pool thing wasn't an accident?"

He didn't respond, just continued to hold my gaze.

Eddie finally let his neutral face slide into anger. "You could have warned us."

James leaned forward. "And you could have told me what was going on."

Eddie shrugged. "Point. But May could have been killed. You should have warned *her*."

I started to shake my head. The last thing I

wanted was for the two big strong men to decide I was the 'little' woman who needed their protection. "I can take care of myself."

To my surprise, James nodded. "I've witnessed that." He finally smiled. "You drive like a pro."

"Wait, that was you chasing us?" I squealed indignantly.

"Of course not," he said. "But you were too busy to notice the third car squealing around the cemetery. Why do you think they didn't follow you out that back road?"

"You cut them off," Eddie said, shaking his head. "I should have known."

Our drinks came. To prove my renegade status, I ordered a slice of pie. In fact, I ordered it so forcefully the waitress blinked in fear.

Or maybe she just had something in her eye.

Either way, I was woman. Watch me eat pie.

"That sounds great. I'll have one too," Eddie said.

"Make mine cherry," James said.

I slumped in my seat, unhappy. I couldn't be a rebel if everybody else was rebelling too.

Then I realized what James was revealing. "You've been following us."

He nodded.

"Did Alex tell you to do that?"

"Not in so many words, no." James shrugged. "But you're right. You two are in danger. I couldn't just sit back and watch you get killed."

The slices arrived, and we all fell silent until the waitress had settled plates in front of us and laid down forks.

"Then who is it?" Eddie finally asked. "Who killed Josh?"

James picked up his fork and took a bite, chewing it slowly without looking at either of us.

I stabbed off the point of my pie and slipped it into my mouth, nearly moaning with pleasure as the sweet, creamy substance filled my mouth.

"James?"

Eddie's friend shook his head, swallowing. "We don't know yet. But whoever it is has a wide reach and deep pockets."

"We need to figure out why they killed him," Eddie said.

James shook his head. "I can make a good guess on that."

My eyes widened. "Will you share that information with us?"

"No."

Eddie went very still beside me. He clearly didn't like being on the outside of things. Especially when we'd been very much on the inside of the threatening and barely cheating death part. I hoped he held it together. I didn't want to have to leave without finishing my pie.

"Let him explain, Eddie," I warned.

Deitz didn't appear to hear me. "You *need* to

share that information," he said in a low, growly voice.

James swallowed another bite of his pie, swiping a paper napkin over his lips. "I would have if I'd known you were investigating this." He leaned across the table, his gaze hostile. "You knew Alex was worried. That's why he had you look into those men. You should have been able to put two and two together."

Eddie skimmed me a guilty glance.

I wasn't too lost in banana cream heaven to miss its significance. "You already knew who the potential killers were?"

"No. I only knew who Alex suspected they might be."

"They?" My pulse picked up. "There's more than one?"

"Unless I miss my guess, you two have been checking into Tomlinson, right?"

Eddie nodded stiffly.

I swallowed my last bite of pie and eyed Eddie's. "You gonna eat that?"

Deitz gave me a disbelieving look.

"What? I was too nervous to eat breakfast this morning."

Eddie shoved his plate my way. "I just don't see Sugar Morellis running Josh off the road with a trash truck. It's not his style. He runs a gangland-style organization. If they wanted Josh dead, he'd have been killed in a hail of gunfire."

I shuddered. I hadn't even realized we had cartels in Asheville.

"If you believe that, you haven't been paying attention. These guys keep a low profile. They run their drugs and weapons through the city and nobody except the police know it. When they kill, they take their victims into the mountains and bury them there. When they steal, they generally do it outside of the state and make sure their victims don't talk about it. This is a whole new breed of gang, Deitz. It's one of the reasons they've been able to stay under the radar for so long."

"And we're talking about them, why?" I asked, sitting back with a sore tummy from eating all of my pie and half of Deitz's. "Why would these guys go after the Mitners?"

"Because they've been courting Alex for years. They want his organization in their pockets to clean up their crimes."

"I thought you said they do all their dirty deeds in the mountains."

James nodded, shoving his empty plate away and taking a sip of his coffee. "Discipline is hard. The organizations are brutal about infractions of the rules. Unfortunately, when dealing with low-level criminal types, mistakes are occasionally made. When that happens, they want to limit the exposure to their organizations."

"But as Eddie and I discussed, they'd need a dirty cop."

James nodded. "Yes."

"Robard?" Eddie asked.

James grabbed the check and stood up. "Robard's a friend of Alex's." He lifted one eyebrow, which I took to mean that Robard was considered off-limits. But I'd been around cops and cop logic all my life, so I was nearly as cynical as my family. "If he's dirty, he'll throw Mitner under the bus to stay out of jail," I told James.

"You're wasting your time looking at Tomlinson," James said.

"You don't know that," Eddie countered.

James placed his hands on the table and leaned down, giving his old college buddy the stink eye. "Yes. I do."

He straightened and started toward the cash register upfront. But, as he left, he got one more shot in. "I've got this, Deitz. Back off. Or you won't like what happens next."

Hooboy! That sure sounded like a threat to me.

I gave Deitz some time to cool down before I said anything. As a result, we were halfway across town before I spoke up. "Um, where are we going?"

He spared me a glance. "We've danced around Tomlinson long enough."

I frowned. "What exactly does that mean?"

"It means..." Eddie turned the truck through a large set of wrought-iron gates and down a tree-lined drive into a parking lot adjacent to a one-story building constructed of pink stone and slate. Even I recognized *The Executive Club*, an exclusive golf course for only the most privileged in the Asheville area. "Um...this is a strange time to play eighteen holes, isn't it?"

He parked, ignoring me. As he turned the engine off, Eddie ran his gaze over the cars in the lot. It snagged on a low-slung yellow two-door convertible that was parked under a tree at the edge of the lot. "He's here."

"Who's here?" I asked with some frustration.

Deitz opened his door. "Tomlinson. I think it's time we took this bull by the horns. Don't you?"

Eddie slammed the door closed on my response.

Not that I had much for him anyway. Lip-flapping probably wouldn't be helpful.

I hurried across the lot after Eddie. "Hold on. What's the play here? This is a private club. They aren't going to just let us walk onto the course."

Eddie strode between a BMW and an Audi, his gaze locked on the Porsche Carrera GT that was angled over two spaces in the shade.

I whistled when I realized what it was. "Argh would wet himself if he saw this car."

Eddie ignored my awe, his gaze on his watch. "He should be coming out any minute now."

"Tomlinson? How could you possibly know that?"

"Because I spent two weeks following him everywhere he went. He's a busy man who keeps to a rigid daily schedule. Especially now that he's lining up donors and supporters for a run at Mayor. He starts very early almost every day with either a round of golf at this club or an hour on the driving range."

"Robard wasn't kidding. You *were* following Tomlinson around?"

"Him. And others."

"Which others?" I asked.

"I spent some time watching Sugar Morellis' organization."

"You think Alex agrees with James that the cartel killed Josh?"

"I'm not sure if he does. But James wasn't lying. Morellis has made some not-so-veiled threats trying to force Alex to help them."

I had a thought that I hated. But it had to be considered. "Is it possible Alex has already helped the cartel, and he's trying to cover it up?"

Eddie's gaze spun my way. "You're implying Alex had Josh killed to shut him up? His own son."

"I don't want to imply that, but it happens, Deitz. You know it does."

He sighed. "I've considered it. After what you overheard at the viewing, Doc Leland would be suspect too."

I nodded.

"There he is." Eddie leaned against the car, crossing his arms over his chest and pointing a neutral expression toward the man striding across the lot in our direction.

William Tomlinson looked to be just over six feet tall and was built like a swimmer, with sinewy limbs, broad shoulders, and narrow hips. The navy *Executive Club* golf shirt and trim khaki-colored slacks he wore fit him as if they'd been made by a tailor. He moved with confidence, his stride long and loose.

Tomlinson's dark hair was cut business short, the cut a perfect frame for his narrow face. The sprinkle of gray on the sides made him look distinguished without making him seem old.

I could easily see why an attractive thirty-something professional woman like Allie Landon would be drawn to him. A young and fit fifty years old, he exuded confident elegance without being too slick.

Tomlinson would probably do well in his run for Mayor if he wasn't in prison for murder.

As he approached, Tomlinson glanced up. His neutral expression turned quickly to irritation as he spotted us. The irritation transformed even more quickly to anger when he saw Eddie leaning against his car. I didn't blame him. The Porsche cost more than many people's homes.

"What are you doing? Get off my car!"

Eddie complied, but he moved very slowly as if he were trying to annoy Tomlinson.

Tomlinson's handsome face turned dark. He shoved past Eddie to the car, running a long-fingered hand over the finish where Deitz had been sitting. "I'm just about over dealing with you reporters. You don't respect anything." He stood nose to nose with Deitz, a pulse dancing visibly in his sun-tanned throat. "If you don't leave me alone, I'm going to get a restraining order."

Deitz lifted one hand and showed Tomlinson a laminated rectangle.

I watched Tomlinson's expression change. "You're an investigator?"

Deitz nodded.

"Who are you working for?"

Eddie shook his head. "That's confidential. I wanted to get your side of things before my client went to the police."

Tomlinson's color faded quickly as Eddie's words took root. "What's this about?"

"We found the knife. I wondered if you wanted to tell us your side of the story before this all blows up."

Tomlinson's color had continued to fade until the

new paleness ate into his healthy, sun-kissed tan. "I have nothing to hide. I didn't kill Allie. I couldn't have killed her. I loved her."

His gaze skimmed to me and confusion filled his expression, but before he could ask about me, Deitz swayed sideways and got between us, forcing Tomlinson to look him in the eye. "Why'd you hide the knife?"

Tomlinson shook his head. "I didn't. I'm being framed."

Well, that was new. "By whom?" I asked.

Tomlinson's attention was drawn back to me. "I'm sorry, who exactly are you people? Who do you work for?"

"I've already told you..." Eddie started.

"Don't bother," Tomlinson said, cutting him off. "I know who you're working for. You're working for her brother."

Deitz didn't deny it, so I spoke up. "Ms. Landon's family believes you knew about the scalpel. That you killed her with it. And then hid it."

He shook his head, looking at the ground between his and Eddie's feet.

"When they check it for DNA, are they going to find your blood and prints on it?" I asked softly.

Tomlinson hesitated.

Got ya! I thought.

But his gaze, when he lifted it to me, was filled with such pain it made my lungs seize.

"I told Collen I didn't hurt his sister. I loved her. What's it going to take to convince him?"

Eddie shrugged. "Proof?"

"I can't give you proof. I wish I could. I swear I didn't know that scalpel even existed. She never showed it to me. I came into her house that night and found her lying in a pool of blood." He rubbed a hand over his mouth, his chocolate brown gaze shiny with unshed tears. "So much blood." He shook his head. "I lost my mind. I tried to pick her up. I was going to take her to the hospital. Then I realized she was beyond help and I sat on the ground, holding her in my arms, just sobbing."

A niggle of doubt wormed its way through my gut. Despite what Collen Landon had said, William Tomlinson surely seemed like a grieving boyfriend. "Did you attempt CPR?"

"No. It wouldn't have mattered."

"Where was the knife when you found her?" Deitz asked.

Tomlinson shook his head. "I don't know. I never saw it."

"What did you think had happened when you walked in and found her?" I asked.

He shrugged. "Robbery? Maybe…" He swallowed hard, giving his head a shake as if to expel the concept of other, more horrifying types of physical abuse. "I never dreamed they'd blame me."

"Why do you think you're being framed, Mr.

Tomlinson?" I asked. "Who would frame you, and why?"

Tomlinson didn't answer my question. His expression lost some of its sadness, and he regained some color in his face. Finally, he sniffled. "I've told you everything I know. You can tell her brother that I'm innocent."

Eddie moved into Tomlinson's comfort zone, holding his gaze. "Did you kill Josh Mitner?"

Tomlinson's expression seemed genuinely surprised. "Josh who? I have no idea who you're talking about."

"I saw you leaving the Mitner home a month ago. Will you deny that you spoke with Alex Mitner about forming a partnership?"

Tomlinson's face seemed to clear. "Mitner...yes. I didn't make the connection." He shook his head, irritation returning. "Am I to be blamed for every death or murder in the city now?" He moved around Eddie and climbed into his car.

The little car started up with a throaty purr that would have put even Betty's perfect engine to shame. Tomlinson didn't leave right away. He fixed Eddie with a hostile glare first. "I intend to find out who killed Allie, and I'm going to clear my name," he said. "I promise you that."

Watching him drive away, Deitz frowned. "Well, that's certainly a different side of him than he showed during the post-murder interview."

"You watched it?" I asked, surprised.

He nodded. "Landon was as good as his word. He sent it over right after we spoke to him."

"Maybe Tomlinson was just numb at the time," I offered. I couldn't help feeling like I'd just witnessed true grief. Though nobody knew better than I did how much good acting could skew impressions.

"Maybe."

"But you don't believe that, do you?"

His frown cleared. "Let's just say I'm skeptical. Mr. Tomlinson's story doesn't add up."

"He could have been framed," I offered weakly.

"He could have. But if he killed her, that would be a pretty handy smokescreen, wouldn't it?"

Yeah, I thought. It definitely would be.

17

I dropped my purse on the table by the door and went to let Shakes out of the Pom Hilton. He bounced happily alongside me as we headed for the door. I'd been a little surprised when Eddie had left without offering to walk Shakes with me. Actually, I was a bit disappointed. But I assumed he'd lost interest in the excruciatingly slow process of perfect potty spot selection.

I could certainly identify. Although, as we stepped out into a beautiful, sunny North Carolina afternoon, I gave a happy sigh.

After all, I could be one of the poor schmoes currently eyebrows deep in entrails and brain matter collection.

I shuddered.

Shakes looked up at me and barked happily.

"I know, buddy. You'd probably like talking about entrails and brain matter. That's right up your alley.

My cell rang, and I looked down at it. With a grimace, I hit *Answer*. "Lieutenant."

"MayBell."

Uh-oh. No Punk-in. That was a bad sign. "What's up?"

"You tell me."

A tension-filled silence followed his clipped response. I barely bit back a sigh. "Let me guess, you heard from Detective Robert."

"Why would I hear from him, MayBell? What business could you possibly have with a police detective who's doing his job trying to solve a murder?"

I couldn't hold the sigh back any longer. It didn't even help to see Shakes lift his stubby leg on a tree. "It's not my fault," I snapped my teeth closed on the rest of the sentence. My voice had come out entirely too whiny for a grown woman. "Look, Deitz and I were just walking Shakes last night and Robard pulled up and started harassing us."

"That's what you're going to go with?"

"Yep."

When an unamused silence followed, I added a bit to my response.

"It's the truth."

"He just happened to see you on the street and stop to question you about a murder that happened in Asheville, which you, MayBell Ferth, actress and fake mourner, have no business getting involved in?"

"I know you can sniff a lie a mile away. Why would I risk lying to you?"

It was a good question. And, also, a great dodge to the question he'd asked *me*.

Unfortunately, the Lieutenant is much smarter than the average bear. "Nice try. Tell me why you and Deitz have been snooping around Allie Landon's murder."

I thought about it for a beat, trying to decide if it was worth the grief to come clean, and then decided I really had no choice. "Because we think it's somehow tied to Josh Mitner's murder."

He expelled air into the phone lines. I waited for him to gather his wits about him, visualized him counting to fifteen in an effort to remain calm. In my mind, I saw him scrub a big hand over his no doubt prickly jaw before answering.

He was pulling out all the stops.

Finally, I couldn't stand it anymore. "Lieutenant?"

"Did I not tell you to stay away from the Mitner thing?"

"You did, but..."

"Did you not promise me you would?"

"I think so, but I..."

"Are you a police officer, May? Did you go to the academy and get your badge without me knowing? If you did, I'm going to be mighty peeved because I would have wanted to be at your graduation. You wouldn't deprive me of that, would you, May?"

Not a *Punkin'* in the bunch. He was really ticked. "Look, Dad, I..."

"Did I not warn you about that Deitz character? What is this, some late-blooming rebellious stage that features having a fling with a bad guy type? Because, May, if that's all this is, then stop it! And if you must indulge in bad boy worship, at least find one that's bad in a less dangerous and illegal way."

I frowned. "Dad, I'm thirty-three years old."

There was a beat of hesitation and then, "So?"

"So, I'm old enough to make my own decisions and go against your wishes. I'm an adult, Dad."

"You're not acting like an adult."

"I most certainly am. I'm actually acting very much like an adult. It's an adult thing to want to help when you see someone hurting or to ask questions when something doesn't add up. Just like it's an adult thing, when one finds oneself in danger, to try to find a way out of it."

The quality of the next beat of silence was different. I immediately realized my mistake.

"Are you in danger, May?"

I closed my eyes and hung my head. I'd let the cat out of the bag. And it was a really big dang cat. Bobcat sized. "It was just a figure of speech."

"No. No, it wasn't." There were sounds of movement. "I'm coming over there."

"No! Dad, don't come over here."

"Why not?"

"Because I was just leaving."

"Good. You can come by the house."

I thought fast. "No, I can't. I have a..." I pulled a face. "A date."

"At two in the afternoon?"

"Yes. We're going to the zoo."

I had no idea where that had come from. I hadn't been to the zoo in years.

"I'll call your brother and see if he can double date with you."

"Oh no, you don't!" I surprised even myself with the outburst. I'd never spoken to him that way. But I was desperate. And truth be told, I was a little sick of being treated like a stupid little girl. "I promise you that I'm trying to do the right thing. I'm not breaking any laws, and neither is Deitz." I crossed my fingers on that one. I really didn't know if he was breaking laws or not. "I need you to trust me on this, Dad. Trust me to act like an adult and do the right thing."

"If Robard comes to me again and tells me you broke the law, I won't be able to save you, May."

I nodded. "I understand."

Silence. I chewed my lip, fighting the urge to apologize and capitulate. I hated disappointing the

Lieutenant. But he really needed to learn to stay out of my business.

"Fine. I'll step back and trust you. But that doesn't mean I won't worry about you."

I breathed a sigh of relief. "I wouldn't want it any other way. I love you, Dad."

He hesitated a beat, and I was afraid he wasn't going to say it. Finally, "I love you too, Punkin. You take care now."

"I will."

I disconnected to the rhythmic sounds of Shakes horking up grass under a nearby tree. I crouched down beside him and scratched his back. "Is your tummy upset, little man?" His response was to hork up some more grass. Though he did give his tail a little wag.

I straightened up as a distant thought slipped through my brain, too pale for me to grasp. After a minute, I gave up. It wouldn't come to me. Giving a mental shrug, I tugged Shakes' leash gently. "Come on, little man. Time to head home. I need to hit the grocery store so we have something to eat for dinner."

As we approached my apartment building, a woman opened the door to a car sitting at the curb and climbed out.

I recognized the woman. I also realized I wasn't going to make it to the grocery store after all. I smiled at Valerie Mitner even as my mind spun with questions about why she was there. "Mrs. Mitner. It's nice to see you again." I struggled to remember what Ruthie's instructions had been about dealing with a client after the obligation had been met. Somehow, I didn't think Valerie was there to ask for more services, but I couldn't imagine why else she'd come.

Val Mitner's eyes were wide, and her lips were formed in a taut line. She seemed even more upset and nervous than the last time I saw her. "I've come to warn you."

I blinked. I hadn't been expecting that. "Would you like to come up? I can fix us some tea. Or coffee if you'd prefer."

She shook her head, her hands gripping the edge of the window on her car door. She didn't even step all the way out of the car and close the door. She appeared to be ready to leap back inside at a moment's notice. "I won't be here long. I wanted to tell you that you need to watch out for Leland."

I blinked, trying to remember where I'd heard the name before. "Leland?"

"Doctor Leland. He works with my husband." She frowned. "I think they're up to something at *Crime Clean,* and it's not good."

I had so many questions. "Are you sure you don't want to come upstairs? Just for a short while?"

"No! Listen to me. You're in grave danger!"

"Okay, I'm sorry. I won't interrupt again. Tell me why you think I'm in danger."

"I don't *think*, girl, I *know*. I heard them. They're plotting to get rid of you. Leland didn't finish the job that night, and he's determined to do it."

Something cold and creepy clawed its way up my back. "Finish the job? Are you saying...?"

"You were pushed into that pool, weren't you?"

I flapped my lips a few times before I could get the words out. "Did you see it?"

"Not the actual pushing. But Leland was out there a few minutes before you went into the water. I saw him talking on the phone."

I cast my mind back, trying to remember what I'd been doing. Had he heard Deitz and me talking about them whispering at the funeral? And if he had, would he have tried to kill over it?

"Why would he want to kill me?"

She shrugged. "Leland's convinced you know something. I don't know what he thinks you know. But he seems determined to shut you up."

I swallowed hard. "Did he say those words? Shut me up?"

She nodded. "Anyway. I didn't want to get involved, but I've been a wreck worrying about it. You deserve to know. She slid back into her car and hesitated before closing the door. "Stay close to Eddie. He's a good boy. He can keep you safe." She slammed the door without another word and sped away.

Shakes and I stood on the sidewalk, staring after her.

My beautiful sunny day had gone cold and ugly.

———————

"You sure you want to do this?" Deitz asked me for about the tenth time. "I can talk to him alone."

I glanced at him, making a herculean effort to smooth out the frown I'd been wearing since speaking to Val Mitner. "I need to be there. I need to look him in the eye and give him all the reasons why he doesn't want to mess with me." Brave words, coming from someone who was having trouble keeping her knees from knocking together.

Deitz didn't look convinced, but he nodded. "Okay. Let's go then."

Eddie had been able to locate Doc Leland's home address, and we went there first. A woman with faded gold hair answered the door, eyeing us with hostility. A couple of quick questions deter mined that she was Leland's housekeeper. And she succumbed enough to Deitz's charm to tell us that the doc was down the street at the *Farmer's Market*.

"Picking up peaches," the woman told Eddie with a smile. "For my peach cobbler."

Deitz grinned. "My favorite. Especially with fresh peaches."

Her smile widened and gained a slightly leering quality. I suddenly felt like a third wheel on date night. "I do," she responded. "No canned peaches for *my* cobbler." Her eyebrows waggled suggestively.

I couldn't help thinking that Deitz had better watch out or he was going to become the woman's next "peach."

"Have you been the doc's housekeeper for long?" I asked, just to pull her attention off Deitz.

Her smile tipped upside down when she looked at me. "Almost ten years. You won't find a better man than Doctor Leland."

"He has an exciting job though, doesn't he?" Eddie said. "I'll bet he could tell you some pretty gruesome stories."

She shrugged one shoulder, giving the idea only lukewarm interest. "He cleans. I clean. He just cleans different stuff than I do."

Well, that was certainly one way to look at it.

We thanked the woman and started down the steps. But she called out, stopping us. We turned.

She stepped through the door. "You people need to stop harassing him. He's a good man. He doesn't deserve it."

Eddie and I shared a look. "We people?" I asked, frowning. "What do you mean?"

Her upper lip curled slightly. "Don't think I don't know who you are. My husband came from Mexico. He told me stories about the stuff the cartel pulled down there. I know you're with them. They love the pretty blonde types for cover. But you..." She pointed a finger at Deitz. "You're charming, but you reek of the cartel. You leave him alone. He's no danger to you."

As the door closed between us, Deitz and I shared a surprised glance.

"What in the world?"

We tried knocking on the door again, but the housekeeper had apparently said her piece and wouldn't open it again.

Fifteen minutes later, we were rounding a table of cantaloupes and watermelons in search of a short, balding forensic pathologist.

I spotted him a minute later, haggling with a tall, ginger-haired woman over an enormous head of cauliflower. "There!" I pointed at the doc. Deitz and I hurried through the crowd toward him.

By the time we arrived at the cauliflowers, Doc Leland was gone. The tall, ginger-haired woman smiled. "You want a head of the best cauliflower in the city?"

I shook my head. "Maybe later. Did you see where that man who was just here went?" I held a hand a couple of inches above my own head. "About this tall and balding."

The woman shook her head. "Sorry. I've been busy."

Deitz and I turned away and plunged back into

the crowd. It was a big crowd, made even more over-whelming by the abundance of tables filled with stuff that everyone needed to navigate.

I finally saw a long table filled with fresh peaches and grabbed Deitz's arm. "Over there."

Leland was carefully examining a fat, perfect peach as we approached.

"Doctor Leland?"

His gaze shot up, narrowing on us as if he was trying to remember who we were. "Ah, Mr. Deitz and Miss…" He shook Eddie's hand and looked at me.

"Ferth," I told him. *As if he didn't know*. I crossed my arms over my chest to discourage him, in case he tried to shake my hand too.

"We need to speak to you for a minute. Is there someplace quiet?" Eddie asked.

Leland hesitated, seemed about to ask us what we wanted to discuss, and then nodded. "This way." He led us to an area just outside the market and indicated a series of stone tables with attached benches. I picked the table that was farthest from the crowd, and we sat down.

"What's this about?" Leland asked.

Eddie took the lead, which was fine with me. Finding myself face-to-face with the man who might have tried to kill me that night at the Mitner's was proving more unsettling than I'd thought it would be.

"We've been told that you were in the vicinity of

the pool the night May was pushed into the water. Did you see anything or anyone nearby?"

I was watching Leland carefully and saw the slight tightening around his eyes that screamed guilt. Still, he shook his head, feigning disinterest. "No. I'm sorry, I wasn't there."

"We have a witness who can put you on the patio," Eddie insisted.

Leland's mouth moved as if he were chewing over a response. I could tell his instincts were to keep lying, but he wasn't stupid. If he was the one who'd pushed me into the pool, lying would only make him look guiltier.

"Okay, you're right. I was out on the patio. But I was on my phone and not paying attention. Then the lightning started, and I ducked inside. I'm afraid I didn't see anything." He looked my way. "I'm sorry."

Eddie hesitated a moment, letting Leland's insincere apology hang between us like a rotting apple on a bug-infested tree. Then he leaned in, lowering his voice. "Doctor Leland. Our witness also heard you threatening Miss Ferth."

To his credit, Leland was a very good actor. He'd have given some of my colleagues in community theatre a run for their money. His mouth fell open. He gave me a look of pure horror. "That's not possible. I'd never..." Then his look turned dark. "Who is this witness? I'm being framed."

Okay, that seemed a bit over the top. Not to

mention a bit repetitive since I'd heard that excuse from one suspect already. I shook my head. "We're not telling you that. If what the witness says is true, you might try to hurt them."

"I've never hurt anyone in my life!" His anger seemed to deflate a beat later as Deitz and I continued to stare at him. "Look, I can see why you'd think that, my being on the patio when you were nearly killed..."

"What did Miss Ferth do that had you thinking about killing her?" Eddie asked, his tone hard and cool.

Leland's shocked gaze slipped back to me and gained a pleading quality. I hardened myself against it, firming my lips and staying silent.

Finally, he sighed. "It's all a big misunderstanding. I wasn't suggesting we kill her. I'm not a violent man."

"Then what *were* you suggesting?" I asked quietly.

"I saw you snooping at the viewing. I thought you'd overheard..."

"Overheard what?" Eddie asked.

"That's not important. But I need to make something clear..." He leaned close and I scooted away before I could stop myself.

Eddie reached out and grabbed his arm. "Back off, Leland."

He shook his head. "I wasn't going to hurt you,

Miss Ferth," the pathologist said, "I just wanted to pay you off. If you knew about the payoffs..." He didn't finish the thought, but I got the gist of it. I assumed he and Mitner had been bribing Robard for the inside track on scene cleaning. "You were bribing Robard, weren't you?" I asked.

Leland held my gaze for a long moment, his eyes making promises I didn't want to consider. I was guessing he was silently offering another bribe. To me.

He stood and turned back toward the market. "Think about my offer, Miss Ferth. I'll make it worth your while."

Eddie stood up and started after him. "Hold on, Leland, you can't..."

Leland was ten feet away when a shot rang out. Something white and chunky, tinged in red, flew into the air and rained down on the crowd as they screamed and scattered.

Doctor Leland dropped like a rock.

Right in front of the tall ginger-haired lady's table.

18

S creams went up all around us. People ran past in droves, knocking me into Deitz and sending us scurrying behind the stone table for cover.

When a moment had passed and no more shots rang out, Deitz looked at me. "Stay here."

I watched helplessly as he scooted out from behind the table and ran toward the prone body on the grass a dozen feet away.

The market was silent as everyone waited for the next shot.

It never came.

Deitz checked on the ginger-haired lady, crouching behind her table, and then asked loudly if everyone else was okay.

Someone yelled out that they'd called 911.

Deitz dropped to his knees next to the fallen pathologist.

Despite the thundering aspect of my heart that seriously made me feel like I was going to pass out, I ran toward Deitz, my movement spurring the rest of the curious. People slipped out from behind trees, rocks, and tables to see about the man on the ground.

A fast, rhythmic whomp sound entered my awareness and then got lost behind a roaring sound in my ears.

Squeezing my eyes shut, I stood several feet away like the coward I was and let Deitz check Leland out. "Please tell me I'm not about to regret missing the entrails and brain matter lecture," I told him.

There was a long, extended groan and I opened one of my eyes. "He's alive?"

Deitz didn't answer. He was busy dragging off his shirt.

I tried not to notice the smooth, golden expanse of his back or the way the muscles rippled beneath the skin as he folded the shirt and wrapped it around some part of Leland's body.

In the distance, sirens sounded, growing rapidly nearer.

The silence in the market seemed louder than those sirens. "Deitz?"

I peered at Deitz's broad back, seeing only Leland's small feet and short legs, unmoving, on the grass. My gaze resisted the painted white chunks all around him. I was really afraid to know what it was.

"It's just cauliflower," a voice said next to me.

I jerked around but realized the young man wasn't talking to me. He was telling his pale-faced girlfriend. She was standing with her hands on his shoulder, looking terrified.

"And peaches," someone else said.

My hair started to blow around my face. I gathered it into my hand, holding it away from my face so I could see.

One of Leland's legs moved.

Deitz reached out and placed a hand on him. "Lie still. The bullet just grazed your head. You'll be fine, but you're going to have one heck of a headache."

Leland groaned as if to support Deitz's observation.

I forced my feet to move forward. Standing next to Deitz, I looked down. "Who shot you?" I asked the fallen man, not realizing until the words came out how ridiculous they were. The chances of Leland either knowing that or telling us if he did know were slim to none.

Deitz reached up and tugged me down. "Stay low. Just in case."

Murmuring started in the surrounding crowd at his words and, moving as one, the whole circular mass of people stepped back a few feet.

The movement left me feeling very exposed.

The wind picked pieces of debris up off the

ground and pelted us with it. I tugged on a small stick that got stuck in my hair.

My cell rang and I didn't even look as I answered. I knew who it was. "Hey."

"May, what have you gotten yourself mixed up in?"

I was only slightly relieved it was Argh and not the Lieutenant. "Deitz and I were at the Farmer's Market and…"

"I know where you are. Your pale, clueless mug's been all over the news. Dad's biting his teeth off one at a time and spitting them at us."

The rhythmic whomping sound I'd been ignoring suddenly loomed larger, and I looked up into the source of the growing wind. A chopper bearing the letters WLOS on its belly hovered overhead, a man with a camera hanging out the side door.

"Great."

The sirens screamed to a stop in front of the *Farm to Table Farmer's Market*. The police jumped out of their squad cars, guns drawn.

"I'd better go talk to them," Deitz told me. He moved through the crowd and, lifting his hands into the air, approached the police, calling out the situation as they ran up and frisked him.

I looked down at Leland and twitched in surprise when I saw his gaze staring into mine. Eddie's shirt was wrapped around the older man's head, and there was already blood soaking through the cotton. Leland's mouth opened and moved.

He seemed to be trying to tell me something.

I moved closer but still couldn't hear. I dropped to my knees next to him and lowered my head, putting my ear close to his lips.

He groaned softly and his eyes closed. I thought for a minute that he'd gone unconscious again. But then he ground out the words, "Security... get...security."

"Move out of the way, Miss Ferth."

Looking up into Robard's hostile face, I couldn't help wondering what he was doing there. I stood and moved several feet away.

Robard watched the EMS personnel remove Deitz's shirt from Leland's head and examine him, checking his pupils, blood pressure, and heart rate before moving him.

I stood next to Deitz while the emergency responders worked. Eddie was wearing a bright orange *Farm to Table* tee shirt someone must have given him. "Nice," I said, tugging on it.

He grimaced. "I'm like a beacon for the shooter."

Because I came from a long line of cops and was therefore well-versed in the use of humor as a means of coping with stress, I took two very deliberate steps away from him.

I was happy when his handsome face softened into a grin.

Robard strode over. "Tell me what happened."

We told him—even the part where we were questioning Leland about trying to kill me. We gave up Mrs. Mitner because we had to. Leland could have very easily gotten killed and, if our questioning him had something to do with that, we owed it to the man to tell the police what we knew.

Robard noted everything we told him and then gave us a sour look and told us to stay available in case he had any further questions. I put my hand on his arm as he started to walk away. He glowered down at it until I removed my hand.

"Leland told us he and Mitner had been bribing people for business. You wouldn't by any chance know something about that, would you, Detective?"

Robard didn't speak. Instead, he jerked his head to a spot several feet away, where there were no bystanders and no police.

Deitz gave me wide eyes as Robard turned his back on us, and I shrugged.

I was getting tired of tiptoeing around and putting myself and everybody else in danger.

Robard whipped around as we joined him under a big, old tree near the street.

He jammed a finger toward me, his eyes narrow and tight with rage. "You've got a lot of nerve, *actress!*"

I didn't flinch. I'll give myself kudos for that. But his inflection on the title was clearly meant to remind me that I wasn't a cop. Heck, I hadn't even played one on TV. "It's a question that needs to be answered."

"I don't owe you any explanations. In fact, I've been told that you aren't supposed to be sticking your nose into this investigation in the first place. Your father..."

"You let me worry about my father, Robard. Did you or did you not take bribes from *Crime Clean* in exchange for sending work their way?"

He glanced at Deitz but, to his credit, Eddie acted like my partner. He stood tall next to me, returning Robard's glower with expectant silence.

Finally, Robard growled out an expletive. "Okay, I'm only telling you two dweebs this to get you off my scent. I don't need you getting in the way of me doing my job."

I lifted a brow.

"I don't know anything about any bribes. What I know is that Alex Mitner's been getting threats from the cartel."

"Why?" Eddie asked.

"Because, as you know, they like to keep a very low profile. That means when they occasionally screw up and do some of their more violent business in a place where they don't want anybody to know, they need somebody to clean up their mess in a way that can't come back to bite them."

"They wanted *Crime Clean* on their payroll,"

Eddie murmured. He didn't act surprised. James *had* already speculated the same.

Robard nodded. "This is a mess you don't want to get mixed up in. These people are dangerous. They'll do anything to keep you quiet."

I thought of the pool and the deadly embrace of the massive tree, backlit by lightning, and shivered. "Was Alex playing ball with them?" I asked.

"No. And that's why they killed Josh."

The words were so stark. So unambiguous. And they hit me like a brick upside the head. "They killed him for what? A warning to his dad?"

"That's what I believe, yes."

"But why not just use their own organization?" Eddie asked. "It can't be that hard to train good forensic cleaners."

Robard nodded. "But they wouldn't have the connections with the police Mitner's people do. And then there's Alex himself. He's friends with a lot of cops, and he understands crime. It's kind of a hobby for him. His knowledge and connections are invaluable."

"So, the whispered conversations May heard between Leland and Alex at the viewing were probably about Alex's little cartel problem," Eddie said.

"And if she'd have acted on that knowledge, she would have endangered what the cartel was trying to build with Alex," Robard responded. "And put Mitner's organization under the type of suspicion that would have killed his business. Even if he's refusing to cooperate with Morellis."

I nodded, feeling suddenly very cold. When we believed Tomlinson was the person who was targeting us, it was scary but not overwhelmingly so. Tomlinson was just one guy. He was a businessman. And though I knew on some level that white-collar guys could do bad stuff, I had visceral knowledge of what the cartel could do. "No wonder Val Mitner is so jumpy."

"Yeah. She has reason to be. If her husband continues to resist, I wouldn't be surprised if they make a play on her next."

I grabbed his arm." You need to protect her!"

Robard jerked free of my grasp. "The police can't protect every citizen who needs it. We don't have the manpower."

"I thought Alex Mitner was your friend," Eddie said.

"We go way back. Sometimes I call for him when I see a particularly nasty scene. He's the best in the business. I respect the heck out of that man. But that doesn't change reality."

When we both glared at him, he expelled a breath. "Look, I drive by there several times a day. I'm keeping an eye on the place. But I'm just baggage at this point. They hired James Thomas. He has the best independent security organization in the city. He'll keep Val safe."

His words reminded me of what Leland had muttered. "Leland told me to get security." I frowned. "Do you think I'm in danger from these guys?"

Robard shrugged. "If they have reason to believe you're a loose end, then yeah. You are. I'd take his advice."

19

"I think we need to talk to James again," Deitz said.

I agreed. "Before we do that, can we go over what we know and what we don't know? My head's spinning."

He nodded. "I know the feeling."

"Good." We were sitting in his truck in the street near the Market. After the ambulance carted off Doc Leland, the crowds had slipped away, and the vendors had closed up shop.

All that was left of the incident were a few chunks of cauliflower nestled in the grass inside a crime scene tape barrier.

One uniformed officer guarded the taped-off area, keeping people from going inside. My concern was less for the place where the bullet had grazed Leland's skull and more for the place where it had left the gun.

"Did they determine where the shooter was standing?"

Eddie pointed toward the three-story brick building across the street. It had a flat roof and one of those old-fashioned metal fire escapes leading to a narrow alley. "Up there. He probably just slipped down the escape and hoofed it through that alley to Market Street."

"How good of a shot would you have to be?" I asked him.

"The distance isn't all that much of a challenge for a rifle with a scope. But there were a lot of bodies between the shooter and Leland. And they were all moving."

I frowned. "There's no chance one of us was the target, right?"

He slid his gaze to my face. I must have looked pretty pathetic because he reached over and patted my hand. "We weren't the target."

"How can you be sure?"

"Because if we were, the shooter was really bad. I mean *really* bad. Leland was a good nine or ten feet away from you and eight feet from me when he was shot."

I chewed the inside of my lip.

"What are you thinking?"

I didn't want to tell him what I was thinking. I'd never felt so insecure before. It seemed like there were forces at work all around me that I couldn't imagine or anticipate. It was a strange and terrifying feeling. "I just need to understand all this. It feels like it's rolling over me, and I don't have a grasp on any of it."

"You need to take back some control. I totally get it. Let's go over what we know and try to pull it into a shape we can understand." He inclined his head. "If we believe Robard, then Josh was most likely killed because of something his father was doing that probably had nothing to do with him."

"Okay, if we go with that, then why was he talking to Collen Landon about his sister's murder?"

Eddie thought about that for a minute. "That's a very good question. Maybe he was investigating the murder because he suspected *Crime Clean* was involved somehow. But whoever killed him did it because he was getting too close to the truth."

"The truth about Tomlinson or the cartel?"

"Not sure at this point."

I nodded. "Okay, so let's assume for a minute that Josh and Collen are trying to get the goods on Tomlinson. But only Josh gets killed. Why?"

We thought about that for a long moment.

Eddie sighed. "I go back to something his father was involved in. That's the common thread in this."

"*Crime Clean* does seem to be at the center of everything." I thought about the people I'd met there and had a lot of trouble believing any of them were criminal types. "Do we believe Mitner and

Leland were paying off Robard? Because, if we do, that pretty much takes everything he just told us out of play."

"I believe some of that has happened. But I don't think that's at the center of what's going on with Josh and Allie Landon."

"Okay, let's assume the two deaths are connected. What connects them? James told us the man he saw Allie Landon fighting with at the bar was a businessman. His description didn't sound like a Hispanic man, a.k.a. cartel."

"We should probably clarify that with James. I asked Collen about it, but he doesn't remember that specific incident, so he can't help us. We know Allie had a thing with Tomlinson. Lovers have fights. I don't think that's part of the equation."

"Except James thought Allie and Josh might have hooked up after. That's a connection."

Eddie nodded. "Yeah. That's one connection. And if Tomlinson found out Allie had slept with Josh, that would be a classic motive for murdering both of them. It's really the simplest explanation."

"But it doesn't match what Robard told us," I said, frowning. "And it doesn't explain the machinations between Leland and Mitner. And it doesn't explain why somebody tried to drown me in the pool and run us off the road at the cemetery."

We sat in silence for a long moment, and then Eddie started the truck. "I think we need to talk to

James again," Deitz said. "He's working for Mitner. Maybe he can shed some light on some of this."

I didn't hesitate for long. "I agree."

———

J ames Security was located in a black marble building near the center of town. Its surface shone like glass as we approached, and the people milling around the front door were dressed in black and had duty belts around their waists just like the police wore.

"It looks like James is doing pretty well for himself," I told Eddie.

He nodded. "He's a smart guy who's going with his strengths. He's ex-military, and he worked for the FBI anti-terrorism unit for a couple of years. He's got the chops to back the security gig up."

"Sounds like a good guy to have on our side."

Eddie pulled the door open for me. "It does, doesn't it?"

I slipped inside, stopping to let my eyes adjust to the soft lighting after the bright sun.

"Can I help you?"

The young woman striding toward us wore a crisp black shirt and black trousers that fit her narrow hips and long legs, tapering down to high black boots with a medium heel. Her white-blonde hair was a stark contrast to the unrelieved black, but her pretty face made it all work. She smiled widely, offering me a hand as she approached. "Welcome to *James Security*. I'm Dani."

"Hey," I said as she dropped my hand and took Eddie's." Her sharp green gaze slid over him like a metal detector, seemingly cataloging the level of danger he presented. I hadn't noticed her doing that to me. I was strangely insulted. Did I really look so harmless?

"We'd like to talk to James," Eddie told her. "My name is Deitz. He and I are old friends."

She inclined her head. "Wait here, please."

While we waited, I walked around the small lobby, perusing the photos of James shaking hands with Asheville's Mayor and a few celebrities he must have provided security for. I was impressed by his clientele.

Dani's boots tip-tapped back our way. I heard her a few beats before she emerged from a hallway and approached. "Mr. Thomas is just finishing up a phone call. If you'll come with me..."

We followed her swinging backside all the way down a long hallway to a nondescript door with no plaque. I wondered if that was a security thing. None of the doors leading off the hall had plaques announcing their use.

Dani rapped two quick times and then opened the door, ushering us inside as James was saying goodbye to someone on the phone. She looked at him. "Coffee?"

He nodded as he stood. "Please." James came around his desk and smiled. "May. It's nice to see you again." He clasped my hand warmly, staring into my eyes.

I felt something twitch in my belly, wondering if it was interest or alarm. I wasn't used to being gazed at with such intensity. "James."

The door snicked quietly shut behind us.

Eddie cleared his throat, drawing a grin from James. "Deitz. I didn't see you standing there."

"Har!" Deitz said. "Nice place you have here."

I took a moment, while James was distracted by Deitz, to glance quickly around the room. The office was large and dark, like the rest of the place. One wall appeared to be all windows, but heavy drapes obscured most of the light, leaving only a narrow ribbon of sunlight around the edges to provide a soft glow. The room was pleasantly cool, and I figured that was probably the reason James had the windows covered.

James' desk was oversized, of a highly polished wood that was nearly black. It was centered over a round red rug, which the only spot of color in the room. The floor was covered in gray-washed wide planks, largely unadorned by rugs. I'd have expected black leather chairs, but James surprised with white leather club chairs, conspicuous for being informal in a space that was striving for gravitas.

Aside from the faint glow of sunlight around the curtains, the room was lit by five matching lamps, which were black with plain white shades. They gave off a soft glow that illuminated without being overly bright.

"Have a seat," James told us, indicating the club chairs. "I'm surprised to see you again so soon." His statement seemed directed at me, but we all remembered how he'd left things at the diner, and I knew it was actually meant for Deitz.

"We need you to tell us who might want Leland dead," Deitz responded.

James' square jaw tightened. He held my gaze and, for a moment, I thought he wasn't going to respond. Then he turned to Eddie. "We've already had this conversation."

"The cartel?" Deitz asked.

"If I had to guess."

"You saw the news?" Eddie asked his friend.

"I did." James frowned. "What were you two doing there?"

"Questioning Leland," I told him.

The door opened, and James held up a hand. "Hold that thought."

We talked about the weather while Dani pulled steaming mugs of black coffee off a tray and placed them in front of us. The mugs were black porcelain with the James Security logo in gold lettering.

Very classy.

"Thank you," I told the other woman.

She gave me a pretty smile. "You're welcome." Dani picked up the empty tray and hesitated. "You're Mark Ferth's sister, aren't you?"

Something about the way she said it...or maybe it was the interested glint in her pretty eyes...warned me that the question wasn't just a passing one. Our Miss Dani had stars in her eyes for my brother. "I am."

Deitz looked confused by the obvious question, so I clarified. "Argh."

"Ah."

Dani grinned. "He won't tell me what that stands for. I was hoping you'd give me the inside scoop."

I pretended to be considering the request very seriously. Actually, I didn't need to pretend all that hard. "I don't know if I should."

"Please?" Her slender brows dipped in a pleading frown. "I'll owe you a big favor."

"Do you promise to torture him with it relentlessly?"

Her lips twitched under a barely repressed grin. Lifting her hand, she said, "On my honor and with great pleasure."

"Okay." And I told her.

She left smiling from ear to ear.

"That wasn't what you told me about how he got the name," Eddie said.

I tried not to grin too widely. "I know, but that version will cause him maximum embarrassment. And that's key to every successful negotiation involving Argh."

James chuckled. "This is why I'm glad I don't have any sisters."

I shrugged. "Back to what we were talking about?"

He nodded, sipping his coffee.

"We'd been told by a reliable witness that Leland had decided I was dangerous because I'd found something out I shouldn't have and that Leland was talking about getting rid of me."

James' brows lifted. "Seriously?"

"Do you have any idea what that might be about?" Eddie asked.

"No. I promise, if I did, I'd tell you and I'd put a stop to it." He frowned. "What did you find out that has them so spooked?"

"I wish I knew."

He didn't look like he believed me.

"Honestly," I said, loathe to admit the reason Leland suspected me. It hadn't been my finest hour. "I might have been eavesdropping at the viewing."

James stared at me a long moment and then barked out a laugh. "You were what?"

I explained about trying to leave and hearing the

two men whispering with urgency in the empty viewing room. "I stopped because I didn't want Alex to see me..."

Both men gave me a funny look. "It's a long story. But I kind of stepped back behind a potted palm."

"Oh, May," James groaned. "That's so clichéd."

"I know. But that was the only thing available to hide behind."

"It's true," Eddie said, nodding. "I found her there just before Alex and Leland came out of the room. Leland apparently believes she overheard whatever they were discussing."

"Only, obviously, I didn't because I have no idea what it was."

"And now you're in danger because of something you don't have any knowledge of."

"Yes."

"Do you believe the bullet that took Leland down was meant for you?"

I hesitated a beat.

James noticed. "You're not sure." It wasn't a question.

"Eddie thinks the shot would have had to be really wide off the mark, but with everything that's been going on..."

"He's right. That would be a really inept shooter." James frowned thoughtfully. "More likely it was meant as a warning to Leland to keep his mouth shut."

"I'd like to hire you to protect May," Eddie said out of the blue.

I was so shocked I just sat there blinking.

James stared at his hands. Finally, he said, "I'd be happy to do that, Deitz, but my schedule is booked up months in advance."

"I'd consider it a personal favor."

The two men shared a look filled with some significance I couldn't identify. Clearly, there was something going on I didn't understand. "Deitz, I don't need protection."

He shook his head. "This has gotten way out of hand, May. It's my fault you're mixed up in this mess. I dragged you into it."

Guilt prickled in my chest. "You didn't exactly drag me. I wanted to help."

"But you wouldn't have started down this path without me harping at you."

He was probably right about that. I wouldn't have even considered it. Maybe. "I'm the daughter and sister of several cops, Deitz. I knew what I was getting into. I wanted to help. I still do."

"No. May, he's right."

My gaze shot to James. I hadn't expected him to chime in and agree with Eddie. "Look, James, I appreciate..."

He held up a hand to stop me. "I'll stick close for a few days until Deitz and I can get a handle on what's going on."

"Then you'll do it?" Eddie asked, leaning forward.

James nodded. "You're right. I do owe you. But this wipes the slate. Agreed?"

"Agreed."

"Guys..." I tried again.

"I need to talk to Alex again," James said as if I hadn't even spoken. "He told me he was worried about the cartel...said Sugar had been pressuring him to become their cleaner. But he's trying to resist."

"And it cost Josh his life," Eddie said morosely.

"That seems to be the case, yes," James said. "As you can imagine, Alex won't admit that. He'll have to take responsibility for the death if he does. But it's kind of sitting there like a rotting fish."

We sat in silence for a long moment. I was the first to pull out of my thoughts. "Val Mitner's in danger."

James nodded. "Which is why I wasn't sure I could help you. I've committed to being with her whenever she moves around. I have guys on the house twenty-four seven." He thought about it and then hit a key on his keyboard and examined his computer screen. "I might have someone who can fill in for me with the Mitners." He glanced at me. "What's on the agenda for today?"

"I need to go home and take care of my dog."

"Good. I'll meet you at your place. In an hour?"

I wasn't completely sold on the idea, but it didn't seem like I was going to be able to talk either man out of it, so I nodded.

It was going to be fun explaining James' presence to my family.

20

D eitz walked Shakes with me before he left to "check out a few things."

I didn't question him because I was happy to be left alone with my dog for a little while. I used the time to catch up on a couple of phone calls, one of them to Argh in an attempt to gauge how mad the Lieutenant was about my recent foray into vegetable murder.

I hadn't heard a peep from the old man. That was concerning.

Extremely concerning.

"On a scale of one to ten, how mad is dad right now?" I asked my brother when he answered his phone.

"You can't count that high."

I expelled air. "I was afraid of that. Should I go over there?"

"I wouldn't. At least stay away until the steam stops coming out of his ears."

"Okay. I'll give him a couple of days. Have you heard anything about Leland?"

"He'll be fine. It was just a graze. He was lucky." Argh paused just long enough to give his next words maximum effect. "But the cauliflower was announced shred on the scene."

I chuckled, despite how bad the joke was. Argh had that effect on me. He got me and my corny sense of humor. "I heard it was a *head* shot."

"All the other vegetables are stewing about it."

"Ugh, Argh."

He laughed. "I know. It's not my best work." There was a beat of silence, and I knew he was setting aside the 'Make May feel better" shtick. "Are you okay? We're worried about you. Dash and Sasha wanted to take turns guarding you."

"That's not necessary. I've got James Security coming over here in a few minutes. James is going to stay with me for a couple of days. Just until they get this mess sorted out."

Argh whistled. "I'm impressed. You must be making better money than I thought in that acting gig of yours."

"Not hardly. He's doing it as a favor to Deitz."

"Well, I don't trust that Deitz guy. Plus, he has terrible taste in cars."

"Right?" I agreed.

"But I can't fault him for protecting you. Stay safe, sis."

"I will." The doorbell rang. "I've got to go. My bodyguard's here." I grinned when I said the word *bodyguard*. It seemed surreal.

James and Doug were having a face-off when I opened the door. James' nostrils were flared. "I smell an illegal substance."

Doug frowned. "Dude?"

I waved. "Hey, Doug."

"Dude."

I tugged James' arm, pulling him into my apartment and closing the door. "He gets seizures," I told him. "He's got a doctor's note."

James shook his head. "Does he only know that one word?"

I frowned, trying to remember. "No, I think he knows other words. He just likes that one best. He imbues it with several meanings, depending on the inflection. It's an art form, really."

"Yeah," James said. "I am Groot."

I grinned. Since I was a sci-fi movie aficionado, I got the reference to the tree alien who used those three words as his entire vocabulary. "I am Groot?"

"Sure, I'd love some water," he responded.

I handed him a bottle of water and grabbed one for myself. Then we were standing in my kitchen, staring at each other, and I felt kind of at a loss.

"What do you want to do?"

I shrugged. It felt weird not having something planned. If I were alone, even doing my nails would be an event.

But I wasn't alone. And I was deeply cognizant of the fact that James was a busy man and I was clogging up his time. I suddenly wished I was alone. "Did you get a chance to talk to Alex Mitner?"

"I did. His story hasn't changed. He still believes the cartel is after him and that he and his wife are in danger."

"If the cartel's after him, I'm sure they *are* in danger." I dropped into a chair at my small kitchen table. James drank some water and then wandered over to the window, glancing outside and then both directions along the street.

"Do you believe Tomlinson killed his girlfriend?" I asked.

James turned back to me. "No."

"Why not?"

"Because Tomlinson is about to become our next Mayor. He'd be stupid to do something like that. Whatever else William Tomlinson might be, he isn't stupid."

"Do you think he'll win?"

"He'll win. Well, if he doesn't go down for murder. He's done a lot of good things for the city of Asheville, and he's got lots of connections with the Department of Education and other government agencies."

"You sound like you kind of admire him."

"I do. He's made himself wealthy and important. I respect that."

We sat in silence for a moment. Then my mind slid back to Allie Landon. "If Tomlinson didn't kill her, who did?"

"That's the million-dollar question, isn't it?" James said.

"Okay," I said, grinning. "Tell me what debt this bodyguard gig is paying off?"

"With Deitz?"

I nodded.

"He helped me with something for my sister once."

"Helped? As in investigated?"

"Yeah. She was getting in deep...romantically... with a guy I knew was bad news. But she wouldn't listen to me. So, I asked Deitz to investigate the skunk."

My grin widened. "I take it your intuition was right?"

"Dead on. Turned out he was a small-time thief."

"Did she listen to Deitz?"

"She did. Good thing too. A week later, the skunk in question was killed during a robbery. It was fortunate there was some air between her and him, or she might have been dragged into it."

I winced. "Yikes!" Taking a big sip of my water, I grimaced as nausea rolled through me. I realized I was probably hungry. I hadn't had much to eat. My thoughts stopped, sharpened, and I suddenly knew where the missing weapon in the Tomlinson case was.

"What is it? Is something wrong?"

I shook my head, surging to my feet. "No. Something's very right. Do you know where Allie Landon lived?"

James narrowed his gaze. "Why?"

"Because I think I know where the killer hid the knife."

I texted Deitz as we pulled past the short concrete driveway of Allie Landon's home and parked up the street a ways. I glanced at James.

"No sense advertising that we're here," he told me.

I climbed out and looked around. The houses in Allie's neighborhood came in all styles, shapes, and sizes. But the two things they had in common were the fact that they were very close together and the yards were mostly well cared for, featuring a riot of color with flowers and flowering bushes of every kind.

Allie's home was a low-slung stucco house with a Southwestern flair.

The front entrance was wreathed in climbing

flowers that snaked over the pillars and across the small roof covering the tiny front porch.

A short stucco and brick wall separated the porch from the vibrant line of bushes planted around it.

Deitz didn't respond to my text, so I slipped my phone into my purse and climbed out. "Nice house."

James glanced at me, looking worried. "I don't have a key to get inside."

I wasn't concerned. "That's okay."

He followed me toward the house, his head swiveling to take in our surroundings. I could tell, watching him, that he was a good bodyguard. His gaze was always moving, looking for potential trouble.

I walked up to the porch and stopped, my gaze sliding to the front door, which was ajar. The wood of the door frame was splintered. "Uh, James."

He took one look at the door and pulled a gun from the small of his back. He tugged me behind him. "Stay close," he whispered. "Don't get separated."

I nodded and followed him into the house, taking baby steps to stay as close to him as I could without tripping over his feet.

I sucked in a gasp when I saw the condition of the house. It had been trashed.

The beautiful furniture was lacerated and overturned. The floor was littered with stuffing, along with the remains of several slashed paintings.

I could tell, beneath the destruction, that it had once been a beautiful home. "Such a shame," I murmured.

James cleared the first room and motioned toward the stairwell wall. "Stand there. Keep your eyes open."

I nodded, pressing my back against the wall. As I moved, bits of broken porcelain and glass crunched under my feet. The Spanish-style tile was covered in the stuff. Somebody had had a field day in Allie Landon's home.

A few minutes later, James rejoined me in the entryway. He slipped his gun back into its tidy little spot inside the waistband of his slacks. "The house is empty."

"Who would have done this?"

He shrugged. "Somebody might have tossed the place looking for that weapon."

I nodded.

"Or it could have just been kids. There are signs that somebody might have slept here. With the murder so prominent in the news, everybody knows the house has been empty."

I sighed. "Sometimes I hate people."

He nodded. "Let's look for the knife. I'll need to call this in to the police."

I nodded, pointing to the door. "Out here."

He frowned. "Outside?"

"Yeah. Remember, there was some conversation about Tomlinson being inside for almost twenty minutes before coming outside and horking into the bushes?"

I went back outside and glanced toward my right. The home was angled to partially block the view of the house next door. But when I looked to my left, I could easily see the front porch of the house. And it wasn't that far away. "I'm guessing that's where the neighbor lived who reported seeing him out here."

James didn't respond.

I glanced over the short wall, down behind the thick row of glossy bushes that had grown almost up to the top of the half-wall. "If he came out the door to throw up, not wanting to do it on the crime scene…" I leaned over the part of the wall almost directly in front of the door and acted out the retching scene. "He probably would have done it here."

"That makes sense," James said. His tone was hesitant as if he thought I was crazy.

But I wasn't crazy. I knew I was right. I straightened back up and motioned for James to join me at the wall. "Look."

I pointed toward a spot a few feet in front of where I was standing. He narrowed his gaze. "What is that?"

I grinned. "It's a porcelain shard from the hallway. You can't tell because you can only see a small part of the very top. The soil is soft here from being watered regularly..." I pointed to the telltale black caps in the soil next to the drive. "I took a chance on that, but a lot of the homes in this part of town have sprinkler systems."

He shook his head. "I don't understand."

I couldn't believe how dense he was. Or maybe I wasn't making myself clear. It had been known to happen. "Tomlinson was holding the knife in his hand. When he retched over the wall, he threw it hard. Anybody watching him would have been distracted by the retching and wouldn't have noticed what his hand was doing. Especially with the wall and the bushes muddying up the line of sight."

"Go on," James said.

"Okay, he flings the knife. It embeds itself in the soft soil, or maybe inside one of these bushes. And then he calls the police. They take samples of the contents of his stomach, of course, even though the crime scene is mostly inside. They always consider the vicinity immediately around the home where a murder's been a part of the scene because they just don't know."

"Right. I knew that."

"But they'd have no reason to check the soil here for the weapon. They'd be looking for DNA and surface impressions."

"Still, the chances of the knife being completely buried with one fling are small."

I nodded. "He would have wanted to make sure. After he called the police, he snuck back out here. Making sure he wasn't observed, he'd have moved behind the bushes and pressed it more deeply into the soil. He wouldn't have been able to do that if he didn't have time. The first pitch into the soil was an emergency measure. In case the police showed up too quickly. But when he had time, he made sure it was buried."

I climbed down the steps and shoved in behind the bushes. Starting at the spot where my shard had landed when I fake-vomited, I used my hands to carefully dig around the base of the bushes. My fingertips struck something within seconds. I carefully moved the dirt until I could see the first glint of stainless steel. I glanced up, grinning widely. "Here it..." My smile fell away."

James shook his head. "I really wish you hadn't found that."

An entire collection of really big butterflies erupted into movement in my belly. I swallowed hard. "Um, James, why are you pointing that gun at me?"

He skimmed a glance toward the house next door, melting further back into the shadows of the overgrown bushes. "Just cover that back up and climb on out of there, May. I really don't want to hurt you."

I did as he said, scooting backward out of the bushes and straightening. I made a pretense of shoving my hair out of my face as I looked toward the nosy neighbor's home. *Please let her be peeking out the window.*

"Come on back into the house, May."

I really didn't want to. But I was pretty sure James would use the gun if necessary. Suddenly, his parking a few houses down made perfect sense. Nobody would place him at the house through his parked SUV.

He'd thought of everything.

I scooted past him at the door and moved inside. My gaze slid quickly around the space in the hopes of finding something I could use as a weapon. I really wished I'd pulled that knife out of the ground before I'd showed it to him.

But I'd been so excited about being right.

Stupid May. Stupid.

He motioned toward the living room with the gun. "Have a seat while I try to figure out what to do with you."

I picked up an overturned chair and set it on its legs, testing it first to make sure it would hold before I sat in it.

James pulled out his cell and made a call. He

turned away from me, speaking in low tones as he paced the area near the front door.

I eyed the parts of the home I could see and thought about trying to get to another room. I could lock myself in, blockade the door. Maybe Allie had a landline that was still connected. If I could get a call out to my dad or one of my siblings...

James ended the heated conversation and slipped his phone into his pocket. Judging by the expression on his dark, handsome face, he didn't have good news.

"You don't need to kill me."

"I'm afraid I do."

"I won't tell anybody about the knife, though I have no idea why you're leaving it there if it implicates you for Allie Landon's murder."

"Because it doesn't implicate *me*."

I had to think about that one for a minute. Then it all fell together. The perfect crime puzzle. "That knife incriminates Tomlinson, doesn't it? You're using its existence to pressure him into working with the cartel?"

I didn't realize until that moment that the snippets of his phone conversation I'd heard had been in Spanish. My panicked brain had only been half concentrating on the conversation.

"Smart girl."

"But I don't understand. You did everything you

could to point us toward the cartel and away from Tomlinson."

"Haven't you been paying attention, May? If I'd have told Eddie to look at Tomlinson, he'd have focused on the cartel."

He wasn't wrong. But Eddie was going to be really ticked when he found out how easy he was to manipulate. "Did Tomlinson even kill her?"

"No. And he didn't kill Josh Mitner either."

"You killed them both."

"Unfortunately, yes. And thank you for proving to me why I need to kill you too."

Stupid May. Stupid.

I shook my head. "My family will hunt you down. They know what I was investigating. They'll figure out I was killed because of the Tomlinson case, and they'll find you."

He shrugged. "If that happens, I'll have to take the appropriate measures."

All the blood rushed from my face. He'd kill my family too. I could tell by looking into the coldly handsome features in front of me that he'd kill anyone who got in his way. Easily and without remorse.

"I think you'll have more trouble getting to them than you did me. They're much smarter."

He smiled. It was surprisingly warm. "Don't underestimate yourself, May. Nobody else even got close to figuring out the knife thing. Nobody. Only you. I think you're very smart. And you have a knack for this investigating thing. Too bad you're not going to be able to make use of the talent."

He lifted the gun.

The doorbell rang.

James and I both turned toward the broken front door.

He frowned. The bell rang again. He thought about it for another minute and then grabbed my arm, jerking me to my feet. James pressed the gun against my temple, digging it painfully into my skull. "You don't say anything unwise...get it?"

I nodded, the cool metal digging into my scalp.

"If they ask, you're here to clean up."

I nodded again.

He shoved me toward the door, stopping me just long enough to peer through the view hole at the top. Then he nodded, moving silently to a spot behind the door.

I grasped the handle, pulled it open, and found myself looking at a woman with tangled gray hair and stooped shoulders. She leaned heavily on a cane, her head bowed and the tangled mess of hair falling over her features.

She held a leash in one hand. The leash moved and a strident yip sounded. A small, furry creature launched itself at me, whining desperately.

I grabbed Shakes and pulled him into my arms before I thought about what I was doing.

The old lady's head lifted. I frowned, thinking she looked strangely familiar...

The space behind me shifted, boiling into movement as someone shouted my name. The old woman said, "Dude."

"Down, May!" That was Argh. I shifted sideways and dropped to the ground as shots were fired.

The wood near my head splintered and someone called out.

A hard grip found my arm, wrenching me upward. Shakes flew away from me with a throaty snarl, his tiny teeth flashing toward the offensive grip.

Shakes' teeth sank deep. He leaped up, wrapped his little body around James' arm, and held on as James tried to shake him loose. The tenacious little canine rode out the attempt, his jaw firm on James' gun hand and his short little legs holding firm.

The gun dropped into my lap just as James swung his arm to the side, trying to bash Shakes' tiny body into the wall.

I screamed, "No!" Clutching the gun in desperation, I pulled the trigger. James collapsed toward the ground, screaming and holding his right knee.

A big hand snapped out and blocked his arm, twisting it downward so I could grab hold of Shakes.

"Let go, little man," I said, my voice thick with tears.

Shakes did as he was told, disengaging himself and leaping into my lap to give me happy kisses.

Meanwhile, Eddie yanked James away from us, slamming him to the ground. He put a knee in the center of James' back, holding him down while Argh yanked his wrists together behind his back and cuffed him.

As Argh shoved a battered and bleeding James out the front door, Eddie knelt down in front of my dog and me.

I held Shakes in a death grip, my face buried in his fur, and he was soaked with my tears.

"Are you okay?"

I nodded. "I can't believe you brought Doug in undercover." I grinned through my tears.

Deitz cocked his head. "Dude."

We laughed, and it felt really good as a release to the unending tension of the last hour.

The four of us sat in my father's kitchen. It was me, Eddie, Argh, and the Lieutenant. The three men were getting along better than I'd expected. I figured it was because they were united in one goal. Keeping me out of trouble.

They might need more people.

I would have added Shakes to the mix since he always protected me too, but the Pom was currently draped across my dad's lap, ignoring me.

I grinned.

"What's so funny, Punkin'?" my dad asked.

I shook my head. "It's just nice being here with all of you."

Shakes lifted his tiny head and settled his chin on the table, giving me goo-goo eyes across the table. He still loved me even though his favorite cop was in the room.

We'd been talking over the details of the James bust. I'd just asked Eddie how he'd known about James.

"You know how I told you I had some things to check out before? When James was coming over to stay with you?"

I nodded.

"Well, I went to *James Security* again. I spoke to Dani..."

Argh's attention perked. "Dani Kraft?"

Eddie waggled his brows. "She likes you too. You two should hook up."

"Hey, there!" growled the Lieutenant. "There'll be no talk of hooking up in my house."

We all grinned. Except for my dad, of course. But his fuzzy friend seemed to be grinning too, and Shakes' tail gave a few half-hearted wags beneath the table.

"Anyway, I told her I was interested in hiring the company long-term..."

I frowned. "Really? Why?"

"It was just a ruse. I wanted to find out what kind of arrangement James had with Alex Mitner."

"You thought there was something hinky going on there?" my dad asked.

"I don't know what I was thinking, to be honest. But James had said some things that had my radar up. I wanted to find out who else he was working with. I asked her for a list of current references. I thought I'd find Tomlinson on the list."

"Did you?" Argh asked.

"I did not. Which was almost weirder than if I *had* found him there. James has made his reputation from working with high-profile clients. But the strange thing is his rep just kind of appeared one day. There was no slow build-up. One day he was babysitting a naughty college girl for her worried parents, and the next he was moving into an expensive building and had a fleet of black SUVs."

"He was being backed by somebody with a lot of money," I speculated.

"That's what I thought. And Alex Mitner has money, but not that kind of money. This would take a serious amount of throwaway cash."

"Like the money a drug cartel would have, for example?" my dad asked.

"Bingo." Eddie nodded. "James did a good job of throwing us off his scent. When he met May and me in that diner, he seemed to be protecting Tomlinson. But his story about Allie Landon meeting up with an arrogant businessman in the bar was meant to throw suspicion at the man everybody believed killed her."

"We talked about that, and you said it didn't seem important."

He nodded. "That's what James wanted us to think. That it was just a little spat between lovers. But it led us to the obvious next conclusion."

"That Tomlinson had killed Josh and Allie out of jealousy." I nodded.

"Yeah. And when the knife was found, Tomlinson's goose would be cooked."

"Tomlinson's print *was* on the knife," Argh said.

"He was being set up by the cartel," Eddie said. "If he didn't play ball when he became Mayor, they'd make sure that knife was found."

"Wait," I said. "You lost me. If Tomlinson didn't kill Allie, why'd he hide the knife?"

"He didn't. Your idea of how it got in the bushes was close to the truth but not exactly right. James hid the knife there after he killed Allie because he knew the police would assume the scenario you laid out. That Tomlinson used a show of vomiting to hide it where he didn't think the police would look."

"But if they wanted to finger Tomlinson, why hide it so well?" I asked.

"It was meant to be insurance, in case Tomlinson didn't do what Sugar wanted him to."

"Then, James *did* work for the cartel," I said.

"He did their wet work. If somebody needed to be taken out, he'd do it. That kept all suspicion far away from them. Since there was no record of any association between them and him..."

"I take it he was paid in cash?" my dad asked.

Eddie nodded.

"Those poor people," I said. "Somebody needs to stop the cartels. They're ruining lives."

Argh nodded. "The APD is working on setting up a task force to do just that. At the very least, we'll make sure they have no power over Tomlinson or Crime Clean anymore. Once Morellis understands that if anything happens to any of them, we'll be all over his organization like bees on lavender, he'll back off trying to pressure them."

"Unfortunately, if there's no direct connection between James and the cartel, it'll just be his word against mine that he killed Josh and Allie." Then I had a thought. "Wait, that night I was atta—erm—by the pool..." I risked a quick glance at my dad and found him petting Shakes. I relaxed. He apparently hadn't heard my slip.

"The night you were attacked at the Mitner's," the Lieutenant asked, lifting a stern gaze my way. "Don't play me for a doddering old fool, Punkin'."

I sighed. "*That* night. You were going into the house to look for Josh's phone. Did the Mitner's have it? We got sidetracked, and you never mentioned it."

"No. James must have grabbed it before leaving the scene."

"But we don't need it," Argh said. "We have the phone records for the cell James carried. It shows a call to Josh right before the accident. All by itself, it's not enough..."

"Not quite," Eddie said with a grin. "But, that current reference list I mentioned? It also included a small startup trash company on the Northside of Asheville."

I felt my pulse spike. "You found the truck that hit Josh?"

"He did," Argh said. "And there were minute traces of paint from Josh's car on the bumper. But even better, we have James' DNA from the cab of that same truck."

I grinned. "We got him."

"Yes, we did, Punkin," the Lieutenant said, sharing my grin. "Nice work."

I beamed back at him.

"Never do it again," he said, glaring at Eddie and me.

My smile died a cruel death.

"But why did Sugar Morellis have Josh killed?" I asked.

"We knew the cartel had been pressuring Alex to work with them," Eddie said.

I nodded.

"What we didn't know is that those cash payments we believed were bribes were actually protection payouts. Sugar had been bleeding Alex and Leland dry in an attempt to force Alex to capitulate..."

"Wait," I said. "They were taking money from Doc Leland too?"

"He's a silent partner at Mitner Enterprises," Argh told me.

Eddie nodded. "Those payments are what we think Josh discovered. The large payouts to the Mexican restaurant on the south end of Asheville that was Morellis' base of operations. Leland let it slip when Sugar's goons were strong-arming him one day that he thought Josh saw the ledger and put the pieces together."

"And Josh went to Collen Landon to try to find out if Tomlinson or Allie Landon might have been suffering the same strong-arm tactics," the Lieutenant said. "He was going to bring the whole thing into the open. Morellis couldn't allow that."

"So, Doc Leland was the cause of Josh's death?"

"Unfortunately, yes," Eddie said, nodding.

I shook my head, my heart twisting with pain for the doc. He'd be devastated to learn what he'd done."

The doorbell rang.

Argh surged out of his chair. "Pizza!"

Shakes jumped down and followed Argh to the front door, barking excitedly.

My dad pushed to his feet and hurried after them. "Make sure to give the boy a big tip," he called out to my brother. Left to his own devices, Argh tended to be a stingy tipper.

Eddie and I looked at each other and smiled. He reached out and grabbed my hand, lifting it to his lips. "I can't remember the last time I had so much fun on a case."

I chuckled. "Well, it was my first case, and parts of it were definitely not fun..." I sighed. "But I have to admit it had its moments."

"You're good at this investigating thing, May. If you're ever looking for a change of career..."

A warm flush came over me. Despite the fact that Eddie's words were hauntingly familiar in a bad way since they'd first come from James, they made me feel good.

I hugged the sentiment close for a beat, enjoying the warm mush in the general vicinity of my pride, and then shoved it away.

I was an actor. I loved what I did. And I couldn't see myself ever changing.

I told Eddie as much.

He took it with good grace. "Well, maybe you'll just occasionally want an adventure."

"You'll be the first person I call," I told him.

"Don't even think it, MayBell Ferth!" the Lieutenant boomed, coming back into the kitchen. "You're an actress. Not a danged detective." He moved to the cabinet where the plates were kept, pulling down a stack of them.

"Leave the detecting to those of us who're trained for it," Argh agreed. He came into the kitchen holding two large pizza boxes at chest level to keep the ever-bouncing ball of fluff at his feet from sinking teeth into one of them.

The Lieutenant smacked Eddie on the arm. "Make yourself useful. Get the beers."

"I'll have a diet soda," I told Eddie. "A girl's gotta watch her weight."

My brother snorted. "Yeah, 'cause this is diet pizza."

I shoved him aside as I headed for the napkins. "Unlike you, I don't intend to eat six pieces of it, porcine individual."

He made piggy snorting noises at me.

We settled into the pizza, everybody munching down on their own slice. Even Shakes had a small triangle in front of him and was holding it with his paws, chewing delicately.

The Lieutenant said he was a police dog now and deserved his cut of the booty.

I let him eat it, knowing he'd probably be horking it up on my bed later. Dad was right. He'd earned it.

"Hey, May, what exactly did you tell Dani Kraft about my name?"

I felt Eddie stiffen next to me and threw him a grin. "Mark? Nothing at all. It's just a name, after all. Kind of boring, actually."

"Not *that* name. Don't play coy with me, MayBell Ferth."

I didn't even wince at the full name thing. I didn't need to. My brother didn't have the ammunition he needed to take me down.

I wasn't the one named Argh. "There might have been some mention of your first date with Cindy Paltrose."

He threw up his hands. "You didn't!"

Even the Lieutenant laughed. "Argh!"

I burst into laughter too. "Argh!"

Eddie didn't know what he was laughing at, but he enthusiastically joined in because—well—making fun of my brother was the best entertainment we had at the moment.

And I was happy as a pig in mud to keep it that way.

Argh!

The End

DON'T MISS OUT

Sam doesn't give away a lot of books. But she values her readers and, to show it, she's gifting you a copy of a fun book just for signing up for her newsletter!

SIGN UP FOR SAM'S NEWSLETTER!

https://samcheever.com/newsletter/

ALSO BY SAM CHEEVER

If you enjoyed **Mourning Commute**, you might also enjoy these other fun mystery series by Sam. To find out more, visit the **BOOKS** page at www. samcheever.com:

Country Cousin Mysteries
Silver Hills Cozy Mysteries
Gainfully Employed Mysteries
Honeybun Heat Series
Yesterday's Paranormal Mysteries
Reluctant Familiar Paranormal Mysteries

ABOUT THE AUTHOR

USA Today and Wall Street Journal Bestselling Author Sam Cheever writes mystery and suspense, creating stories that draw you in and keep you eagerly turning pages. Known for writing great characters, snappy dialogue, and unique and exhilarating stories, Sam is the award-winning author of 80+ books.

To learn more about Sam and her work, visit her at one of her online hotspots:
www.samcheever.com
samcheever@samcheever.com

f